CLAWS FOR CONCERN

Mother bears were protective of their young. They attacked anything that came near their offspring. Anyone who stumbled on a cub was well advised to hasten elsewhere before the mother noticed, or risk being torn to pieces.

The last thing Fargo wanted was a clash with a bear. It would take but an instant for him to jump up, grab a low limb, and climb into the pine. Once he was high enough, the she-bear wouldn't be able to reach him. But that meant deserting the Ovaro. He would as soon slit his wrists.

So Fargo went on unwrapping the Ovaro's reins while keeping his eyes on the mother bruin and the smaller version of herself. Both stood there and returned his stare. The reins came loose. Girding himself, Fargo slid the Colt into its holster, then launched himself at the saddle. He grabbed the saddle horn and swung his leg up and over.

The cub squalled.

The mother roared.

And Fargo got the hell out of there.

The mother bear gave chase. . . .

THE
TRAILSMAN

#327

IDAHO
GOLD FEVER

by

Jon Sharpe

A SIGNET BOOK

SIGNET
Published by New American Library, a division of
Penguin Group (USA) Inc., 375 Hudson Street,
New York, New York 10014, USA
Penguin Group (Canada), 90 Eglinton Avenue East, Suite 700, Toronto,
Ontario M4P 2Y3, Canada (a division of Pearson Penguin Canada Inc.)
Penguin Books Ltd., 80 Strand, London WC2R 0RL, England
Penguin Ireland, 25 St. Stephen's Green, Dublin 2,
Ireland (a division of Penguin Books Ltd.)
Penguin Group (Australia), 250 Camberwell Road, Camberwell, Victoria 3124,
Australia (a division of Pearson Australia Group Pty. Ltd.)
Penguin Books India Pvt. Ltd., 11 Community Centre, Panchsheel Park,
New Delhi - 110 017, India
Penguin Group (NZ), 67 Apollo Drive, Rosedale, North Shore 0632,
New Zealand (a division of Pearson New Zealand Ltd.)
Penguin Books (South Africa) (Pty.) Ltd., 24 Sturdee Avenue,
Rosebank, Johannesburg 2196, South Africa

Penguin Books Ltd., Registered Offices:
80 Strand, London WC2R 0RL, England

First published by Signet, an imprint of New American Library,
a division of Penguin Group (USA) Inc.

First Printing, January 2009
10 9 8 7 6 5 4 3 2 1

The first chapter of this book previously appeared in *Silver Mountain Slaughter*, the three hundred twenty-sixth volume in this series.

Copyright © Penguin Group (USA) Inc., 2009
All rights reserved

The Trailsman

Beginnings . . . they bend the tree and they mark the man. Skye Fargo was born when he was eighteen. Terror was his midwife, vengeance his first cry. Killing spawned Skye Fargo, ruthless, cold-blooded murder. Out of the acrid smoke of gunpowder still hanging in the air, he rose, cried out a promise never forgotten.

The Trailsman they began to call him all across the West: searcher, scout, hunter, the man who could see where others only looked, his skills for hire but not his soul, the man who lived each day to the fullest, yet trailed each tomorrow. Skye Fargo, the Trailsman, the seeker who could take the wildness of a land and the wanting of a woman and make them his own.

Idaho Territory, 1860—among the rivers and rocks, only one thing lurks more dangerous than the Nez Perce Indians—gold!

1

The ten canvas-topped turtles rattled and creaked as they wound into the mountains at the lumbering rate of fifteen miles a day. On good days. On days when the going was steep or the weather was bad or one of the wagons broke down, they lumbered less.

The tall rider in buckskins had no trouble keeping them in sight. He was broad of shoulder and slender of hip, with pantherish muscles that rippled when he moved. His white hat, brown with dust, was worn with the brim low over his eyes to shield them from the harsh glare of the relentless summer sun.

His name was Skye Fargo. He wore a Colt and had a Henry rifle in his saddle scabbard and a double-edged Arkansas toothpick in an ankle sheath, and he knew how to use all three with uncommon skill. As a tracker, he was without peer. He also possessed an uncanny memory for landmarks and a superb sense of direction. A lot of folks got lost in the wilds; Fargo never did. A lot of folks couldn't tell east from west or north from south, but Fargo always knew. He relied on the sun and the stars and his own inherent senses, and they never failed him.

Quite often, Fargo used his skills scouting for the army. At other times he hired out for whoever struck his interest. At the moment he was shadowing the wagon train to earn the one thousand dollars he was being paid to find out what had happened to a missing family. A thousand dollars was a lot of money at a time when most men barely earned five hundred a year. Not that

Fargo would hold on to it. With his fondness for whis-key, cards and women—not necessarily in that order—he spent every dollar he made almost as soon as he made it. A friend of Fargo's once joked that his poke must have a bottomless hole, and the joke wasn't far from the truth.

So here Fargo was, astride his Ovaro a quarter mile to the east of the wagons, riding at a leisurely pace and wishing he was in a cool saloon somewhere with a willing dove on his lap, a bottle of red-eye at his elbow, and a full house in his hand.

Fargo had been trailing the wagon train for over a week now. The wagons were filled with settlers, and Fargo wasn't all that partial to their kind. There were too damned many, swarming from the East like locusts, fit to overrun the West with their farms and their cattle and their caterwauling children. As yet only a few areas west of the Mississippi River had become civilized, but give them fifty years and Fargo worried that the un-tamed prairies and mountains he loved so much would become an unending vista of settlements, towns and cities.

Fargo dreaded that day. City life was all right for a festive lark but too much of it bored him. Worse, after a couple of weeks of having a roof over his head and being hemmed by four walls, he got to feeling as if he were in a cage. He couldn't stand that feeling.

The Ovaro pricked its ears and looked toward the wagons, prompting Fargo to do the same. "Damn," he said, annoyed with himself. He hadn't been paying atten-tion, and two riders had left the wagons and were com-ing directly toward him. For a few tense moments he thought that they'd spotted him. But that was unlikely. He was far enough back in the trees that he blended into the shadows.

Fargo didn't want to be seen until he was ready. Rein-ing toward a cluster of boulders, some as big as the cov-ered wagons, he swung behind them and dismounted.

Palming his Colt, he edged to where he could see the riders approach.

The pair were scruffy specimens. Their clothes had never been washed and their hats were stained, their boots badly scuffed. The rider on the left was short and stout, with a face remarkably like a hog's. The rider on the right was big and wide and wore a perpetual scowl on a scarred face only a mother could love. They slowed as they neared the woods and shucked rifles from their scabbards.

Hunting for game, Fargo reckoned. He strained to hear what they were saying, but they weren't close enough yet. He was concerned they would see the Ovaro's tracks, but they entered the trees at a point a dozen yards north of him.

The pair were prattling away, seemingly without a care in the world.

The hoggish one gave voice to a high-pitched titter more fitting for a saloon girl.

"Ain't it the truth, Slag. Ain't it the truth. I don't know how that dirt grubber puts up with it."

"He does it for the same reason any man does," Slag said in a voice that rasped like a file on metal.

"I'd as soon slit my throat as be nagged and badgered and insulted to death."

"You don't have to worry, Perkins. Neither one of us will ever hitch ourselves to a dress."

Slag drew rein and his companion did the same. Both shifted in their saddles and gazed back at the plodding wagons. "Look at them. Like so many sheep. Makes me glad I'm a wolf."

The two men laughed.

"I can't wait to get there," Perkins said. "For me the best part will be the carving."

Slag snorted. "I believe it. Don't take this wrong, pard, but you're twisted inside. To watch you gives me the chills."

"Why, that's just about the nicest thing anyone's ever said to me," Perkins gleefully responded.

3

"It wasn't meant to be. You're spooky, is what you are. You should have been born a redskin. You would fit right in as an Apache or one of those devil Sioux." Slag paused. "Now there's something I never thought I'd say to a white man."

Perkins lost some of his good mood. "You make me out to be worse than I am. And you like to carve, too. You're just not as honest about it as I am."

"The hell I'm not. I don't brag about it, is all. Or wallow in the blood, like you do."

"There are a few with this bunch who could stand to be cut. Take that Rachel."

"Her? She's as sweet as can be."

"I like the sweet ones best."

"I'm glad I'm not sweet," Slag said.

Perkins cackled uproariously.

Lifting their reins, the pair rode on. Soon the vegetation swallowed them and the clomp of hooves faded.

Fargo stayed where he was. He had heard enough to quicken his suspicions. The question now was what to do about it? He wasn't a lawman. He could go for one but it could take weeks to find a federal marshal and bring him back, and by then whatever Slag and Perkins and their friends were up to would be done with.

Twirling his Colt into its holster, Fargo forked leather. He had a decision to make. The people with the wagon train were nothing to him. He didn't know any of them personally. And given his low opinion of settlers, he should rein around and leave. But there were women and children. And there might be a link between this bunch and the missing family.

With a sigh, Fargo reined toward the wagon train. Once he was in the open, he rode parallel with the wagons but stayed a good hundred yards out. Soon shouts told him he had been spotted. Before long several riders came galloping toward him. One yelled for him to stop.

Fargo drew rein and waited.

Two of the three were settlers. Their homespun clothes

and floppy hats marked them as members of the wagon train.

The third man was different. He was like Slag and Perkins: dirty and ill-kempt and bristling with weapons. Of middling height, he favored a Remington revolver worn butt forward on his left hip. He had high cheekbones and beady eyes and a hooked nose that made him look like a hawk.

"We want to talk to you, mister," the hawk-faced man declared.

"You see me sitting here," Fargo said as they came to a stop. "What do you want?"

The settlers smiled in friendly greeting but the hawk-faced man placed his hand on the butt of his Remington.

"I don't much like your tone."

"I don't much care," Fargo informed him. "Unless you have something to say, I'll be on my way."

"We want to know who you are and what you're doing here."

Fargo shook his head.

"You won't say?" one of the settlers asked.

"My personal affairs are my own."

"What if I insist?" the hawk-faced man said, and just like that his gun hand moved.

So did Fargo's. In the blink of an eye he had his Colt up and out. All three of them heard the click of the hammer. "Draw that six-shooter and I'll blow you to hell."

Amazement turned the hawk-faced man to stone. He stared into the barrel of the Colt and his Adam's apple bobbed up and down. "That was mighty slick."

"Get your hand off that hogleg."

Reluctantly, the hawk-faced man splayed his fingers and held his arm out from his side. "I meant what I said. That was about the slickest I've ever come across."

The biggest settler, who looked to be in his forties and packed a lot of beef on his bones, kneed his sorrel closer. "Enough of this, Mr. Rinson. I won't have you threatening everyone we come across." He grinned at

5

Fargo. "Forgive him, mister. He means well. He just wants to protect us and our families."

"Is that what he's doing?"

The big settler nodded. "He works for Victor Gore. Maybe you've heard of him? He used to be a trapper in these parts. Or so he tells us."

"Never heard of him," Fargo admitted. But that wasn't unusual. The height of the trapping trade had been before his time.

"Well, be that as it may, Mr. Rinson works for Mr. Gore. We've hired them to guide us to the Payette River Valley. We're farmers, you see, and Mr. Gore says the valley is perfect for homesteading." The man offered his big hand. "I'm Lester Winston, by the way. My family is in the first wagon yonder. In the other wagons are friends of ours. We're all from Ohio."

Fargo slid the Colt into its holster, then shook. Predictably, the farmer had a grip of iron.

"I take it you have heard that the Nez Perce have been acting up of late?" Lester Winston went on. "That's why I let Mr. Gore talk me into hiring him and his men when we ran into them at Fort Bridger. They are worth their fee if they get us safely through to the Payette River Valley." He stopped. "Have you ever been there?"

"No," Fargo said. The Payette River, yes, but not of a valley named after the river. Which in itself was peculiar, given how many times he had been through this region.

"Mr. Gore says the soil is so rich, our crops will practically grow themselves. And game is so plentiful we won't ever lack for meat." Lester gazed to the northwest, his eye lit with the gleam of land hunger. "We were on our way to Oregon Country, but after hearing Mr. Gore talk about how grand the Payette River Valley is, we changed our minds."

"This Gore must be some talker," Fargo said, and noticed that it caused Rinson to frown.

"He does have a silver tongue," Lester said. "But he's a fine gentleman. The salt of the earth, if you ask me."

"I haven't met many of those," Fargo said drily.

Rinson let out a small hiss of annoyance. "Are we going to sit here jawing all day, Winston? Gore left me to watch over you while he's gone, and I can't say as I like you telling this stranger all there is to know about us. For all we know, he's an outlaw."

"He doesn't look like one."

"Listen to yourself. You can't tell if a person is good or bad by how they look. I say we send him on his way. And if he won't go, we prod him to move him along."

"I don't prod easy," Fargo said.

"Did you hear him?" Rinson asked Lester. "He's not all that friendly. It's best if we're shed of him."

The wagons had stopped. Men, women and children were all staring with keen interest. They were so far north of the Snake River, in country so rugged and remote, that to run across another white was rare.

One woman, in particular, caught Fargo's eye. She was young and shapely and wore a bright blue bonnet that complemented her darker blue dress. From under the bonnet, fine yellow hair cascaded, shimmering like gold in the sunlight. Fargo couldn't tell much else about her from that distance, but what he could tell prompted him to say to Lester Winston, "I'd like to ride with you awhile. Maybe share your supper."

Rinson growled, "Like hell."

Now it was Lester Winston who frowned. "Need I remind you that I am the leader of this wagon train? I'll make the decision, not you."

"Gore won't like it."

"He's not here. And while I'll admit that our safety should be uppermost on our minds, I refuse to think the worst of everyone we meet. We must all be Good Samaritans, Mr. Rinson."

"Good what?"

"Haven't you read the Bible?" Lester asked. "The milk of human kindness separates us from the beasts, and we must never let the flow run dry."

"I'm not all that fond of milk," Rinson said. "And I never learned to read nor write."

7

Winston turned to Fargo. "Yes, by all means, come join us. My Martha won't mind feeding you. And it will be nice to have someone new to talk to."

"Damn it," Rinson fumed. To Fargo he said, "Mister, you have no idea what you are letting yourself in for. Victor Gore is liable to have you stomped into the dirt, and that's no lie."

"I don't stomp easy, either," Fargo said, and gigged the Ovaro. He had the feeling he was about to poke his head into a bear trap, and if he wasn't careful, the steel jaws would snap his head right off.

2

The farmers weren't sheep. They were puppies. Puppies were friendly and innocent and eager to make new friends, exactly like the farmers and their families. They gathered to see Fargo ride up, all of them smiling and kindly and sincere. And bound to get their throats slit if they didn't realize the frontier wasn't Ohio and puppies didn't last long.

Fargo shook hand after hand as Lester Winston introduced him. The lovely young hourglass in the blue bonnet hovered, watching him but too shy to come forward. Fargo had met most of the men and a few of their wives when he suddenly turned and held his hand out to the blonde. "Pleased to meet you."

She stared at his hand as if it might bite her, then timidly offered her own. "How do you do. I'm Rachel Winston."

"Lester's daughter." Fargo stated the obvious as he lightly clasped her warm fingers.

"Yes," Rachel said, averting her eyes.

"You don't have anything to be shy about, as good-looking as you are," Fargo complimented her.

Rachel glanced at him and blushed a deep red. "My goodness. Do you always come right out and say what's on your mind?"

"Sometimes I let this do my talking," Fargo said, and patted his Colt. He said it not so much for her benefit as for the three men who stood to one side, listening and scowling. One was Rinson. The other two were cast from the same mold: hard, cold, armed for bear, their eyes daggers.

"We should be on our way, Mr. Winston," Rinson addressed Lester. "We don't want to fall too far behind Mr. Gore."

"Yes, yes, indeed." Lester raised his voice for the benefit of the other farmers and informed them that they should climb back on their wagons and get under way. "We have five hours of daylight left and we shouldn't waste it."

Ignoring the looks of the three curly wolves, Fargo stepped into the stirrups. When the Winstons' wagon lumbered into motion, he swung in behind it. Winston and his wife were on the front seat; Rachel and a young boy were riding at the back, and she blushed again as he gigged the Ovaro up close and said, "Hope you don't mind my company."

"Not at all." Rachel indicated her sibling with a bob of her chin. "This is my brother, Billy."

The boy, who wasn't more than ten, studied Fargo with keen excitement. "Are you a trapper?"

"No."

"Are you a mountain man?"

"No."

"Are you a cowboy?"

"You ask a lot of questions," Fargo said. "And no, I'm not." Although he had trapped some, and he had worked with cattle, and he did spend so much time in the mountains, he might as well be a mountain man.

"Are you an Indian fighter?"

"Only when they don't leave me no choice."

"What do you do, then?"

Fargo shrugged. "I scout. I track. I go where the wind blows me."

"That must be fun."

"It has its moments."

Rachel patted her brother's shoulder. "That's enough. You shouldn't badger the poor man so."

"I'm just curious, is all," Billy said, and showed Fargo

his teeth. "When I grow up, I want to have a fine horse like yours. What do you call him?"

"A horse."

"No, I mean his name."

"I never gave him one."

"Why not? A lot of folks do. When I grow up I aim to have a nice horse like you and I'll call him Lightning because he'll be the fastest horse there is."

"Billy," Rachel said.

"What? I'm only talking."

Fargo waited for Rachel to say something to him, and when she didn't, he came out with, "Has Perkins been bothering you?"

Amazement caused her jaw to drop. "How on earth?" Quickly composing herself, Rachel blushed anew and said, "I'd rather not talk about him, if you don't mind."

"Your choice."

But curiosity got the better of her. "How can you possibly know a thing like that? Yes, he's been a nuisance, always coming up to me and asking if I care to go for walks with him when I've made it plain I won't and never will." Rachel paused. "Why does he pester me so? Why can't he be a gentleman?"

"You are honey and he's a bear."

Billy laughed, and Rachel did more blushing. "That's hardly fitting talk, Mr. Fargo. Especially in front of a child."

"I ain't no child," Billy said.

Fargo said to her, "You'll run into a lot of men like Perkins out here. This isn't back East, where men are mostly polite and tip their hats to ladies."

"You're polite," Rachel said.

"I get more honey that way," Fargo said with a grin, and damn if the girl didn't blush the deepest red yet. She also grinned, which set his blood to racing. Her golden hair, her smooth skin, that body; she was a ripe cherry waiting to be plucked from the tree and tasted, and he always did like cherries.

"I'm starting to think you're quite naughty."

"That depends on the lady," Fargo said bluntly.

Just then hooves drummed and Rinson came up next to him. "I don't know as I like you talking to these folks."

"I don't give a damn what you like."

"You keep prodding, don't you? But when we meet up with Victor Gore, you'll be leaving us whether you want to or not."

"A regular he-bear, is he?"

"Victor?" Rinson laughed. "He's more brains than brawn. But when he needs muscle, all he has to do is snap his fingers and he has plenty."

"That would be you and your friends?"

"All eight of us." Rinson grinned, lashed his reins and rode on ahead, his horse raising puffs of dust.

Fargo did the numbers in his head. Slag and Perkins were off hunting. Rinson and two others were with the wagons. That meant three more were with Victor Gore. Nine to one, altogether. Not great odds, but he had gone up against worse. He had to be careful, though. Play it wrong and the settlers would be caught in the cross fire.

"I don't think he likes you very much," Rachel commented.

"The feeling is mutual."

"They aren't very nice, Mr. Gore's men. They treat us like we're simpletons. I don't want to have anything to do with them, but Pa says it's only until we reach Payette River Valley."

"What was wrong with Ohio?"

"Nothing," Rachel said wistfully. "We had a small farm, with cows and chickens and a plow horse and some pigs. I loved it there. But Pa hankers after more land and he says Oregon has plenty just there for the taking."

To Fargo it smacked of greed, and apparently he wasn't the only one.

"Ma says we should have been grateful for what we had. But Pa got a lot of other farmers together, and sold our place."

"You don't sound happy about it."

"I had to give up all I knew. I may never see my friends again. Or my aunts and uncles and cousins. Or Grandma and Grandpa." Rachel gazed at the shadowed woods on the slopes above the valley. "Now here we are, in the middle of nowhere with hostiles and outlaws as thick as fleas, or so they say. No, I'm not happy about it. I'd rather be in Ohio."

"Not me," Billy declared. "Out here there are grizzlies and mountain lions and timber wolves."

"What's so wonderful about that?" Rachel asked. "In Ohio we didn't have to worry. I'd rather be safe than end up in some animal's belly."

"That's because you're a girl." Billy turned to Fargo. "How about you, mister? Where would you rather be?"

"In a saloon drinking whiskey and playing cards."

Rachel tilted her head. "Do a lot of that, do you?"

"Every chance I get," Fargo admitted. He admired how her bosom swelled against her dress and the outline of her thighs, and a familiar hunger stirred. He was content to go on admiring her but someone in another wagon shouted something about riders coming, and Fargo spotted Slag and Perkins tearing hell-bent for leather toward the wagons. From the way they kept glancing over their shoulders, it gave the impression they were being chased. But no one came out of the woods after them.

At a bellow from Rinson the covered wagons were brought to a halt. Lester Winston and the other farmers, armed with rifles and shotguns, jumped down.

Slag and Perkins brought their lathered mounts to a halt and were promptly surrounded, with everyone asking questions at once. Rinson silenced them with another bellow.

"Let these two talk, damn it. We can't find out what happened with all of you lunkheads jabbering at once."

"I won't tell you again about your language," Lester said. "You keep forgetting there are women and children present."

"Oh, hell." Rinson motioned at Slag and Perkins. "Out with it. What brought you back on the run?"

"Injuns," Slag said grimly. ▬

"A war party," Perkins said. "Must be thirty or more."

Another commotion broke out, with the farmers voicing their opinions of Indians in general, and concern for their families. Once again Rinson had to quiet them before he could quiz Slag and Perkins.

"Did they attack you? Did they try to lift your hair?"

Perkins shook his head. "My momma didn't raise no jackass. As soon as we spotted them, we lit a shuck."

"That's all that happened?"

"Go to hell," Perkins said. "We weren't about to stick around and be skinned alive, or worse. There ain't a white cuss in this world I'm afraid of, but those red devils are a whole different critter."

Fargo almost laughed out loud. This was the man Slag claimed would make a good Comanche or Apache? Perkins was right in one respect. There was a big difference between him and most Indians. Few Indians were cowards.

Slag was saying, "When he lit out, I did the same. I don't think the redskins saw us, but they might have."

"And followed you back to us?" Rinson said in some disgust.

All eyes swung toward the woods. Rifles and shotguns were raised and a few hammers clicked.

"I wish Victor Gore was here," Rinson said. "But since he's not, it's up to us to deal with this." He shifted toward Fargo. "How about it, mister? Didn't I hear you were a scout? You must know more about Injuns than any of us."

"A little." Fargo wasn't about to tell them he had lived with several tribes at various times.

A farmer named Harvey nervously cleared his throat. "Are we in any danger? Should we circle the wagons to protect our families?"

"It depends on the tribe," Fargo answered. "The Shoshones and the Flatheads are friendly. The Blackfeet and the Nez Perce aren't."

"Which do you think it is?"

"There's only one way to find out." Fargo gigged the Ovaro on past them and made for the greenery. No one called out for him to stop. None of the farmers jumped on a horse and came along. He looked back when he reached the tree line. They were still there, watching. Lester Winston waved.

Fargo set to work backtracking Slag and Perkins. It wasn't hard. They had crashed through the brush like buffalo gone amok. He rode with his hand on his Colt, every sense alert.

The trees were mostly white pine, with here and there some fir and spruce. Higher up Fargo came on ranks of lodgepole pines and ponderosa. The brush consisted mostly of dogwood. Elderberry and occasional thimbleberry helped break the monotony.

Half a mile of cautious riding brought Fargo to the base of a steep slope. Only partially wooded, it didn't offer enough cover to suit him so he reined to the left and circled until he came to a strip of vegetation that ran clear to the top.

With a light jab of his spurs, Fargo started up. He had gone only a short way when he realized how quiet it was. The birds had stopped warbling and the trees were deathly still. It was unnatural. Drawing rein, he scoured the heights. He must be careful not to ride into an ambush.

Fargo hoped it wasn't the Nez Perce. Years back the tribe had been friendly, but then whites heard rumors of gold on Nez Perce land, and now hardly a month went by without word of yet another clash between Nez Perce warriors and the gold-hungry invaders. The Nez Perce had made it known they wouldn't tolerate more intrusions. Open war threatened to break out.

Off to the left a twig snapped.

Instantly, Fargo whipped around, palming his Colt as he turned. The woods were undisturbed save for a bee that buzzed within an arm's length of the Ovaro and caused the pinto to prick its ears and nicker.

Fargo had a decision to make. Should he go on or

15

should he go back? He reminded himself that he was under no obligation to the settlers. The man who hired him was interested only in his missing kin.

To the right a bush rustled ever so slightly.

From the rear came a whisper of movement.

Fargo kept on riding. They had him surrounded, and if he made a break for it, they would be on him before he went ten yards. He willed himself to relax so he wouldn't give away that he knew, but it was hard; at any moment he expected an arrow between his shoulder blades or a lance in his chest. He looked for a spot to make a stand but there weren't any that suited him.

A low limb brushed the crown of his hat. Instinctively, Fargo ducked, and as he did the limb bounced up and down. Since he hadn't bumped it that hard, something else made it bounce. Belatedly, he went to look up. Just as a heavy form slammed into his back, muscular arms banded his chest, and he was bodily torn from the saddle.

The ground swept toward his head.

3

Fargo twisted to absorb the fall on his shoulder. He still hit hard, what with the weight of the warrior on his back. The world swam and fireflies flickered before his eyes. He felt hands on his wrists. Other hands shifted him to get at his holster. His head abruptly cleared and he looked up into a ring of unfriendly faces. They were Nez Perce. "Damn."

Four young warriors and an older one ringed him. Fargo tried to rise and discovered his wrists were tied. "Do any of you speak the white man's tongue?" he asked.

None of them answered.

Fargo was lucky in one respect. They weren't wearing war paint, which told him they were a hunting party, not a war party. Evidently they were tracking Slag and Perkins when he came along. "I'm not your enemy."

The warriors went on staring.

Like most tribes, the Nez Perce favored buckskins. Although they lived in the mountains, they often traveled to the plains after buffalo, and lived much as the plains tribes did. They were famed for their horse breeding. The Appaloosas they raised were highly sought after. Bigger and heavier than most Indian mounts, Appaloosas were noted for their stamina, and were as surefooted as mountain goats. Fargo got to see five of the famous horses for himself when one of the young warriors went off into the trees and came back leading them.

"You're taking me somewhere," Fargo said, relieved they weren't going to kill him outright. Then he switched to their tongue. He wasn't as fluent in it as he was in some other tongues, but he knew enough to say, "I am friend."

That got their attention. They studied him anew. The old one leaned down, looked him right in the eyes, and said in English, "No white man friend to Nimi'ipuu."

"So you speak the white tongue," Fargo said.

"Missionaries," the old warrior replied. His craggy face was seamed by age and experience, and his hair, which hung in braids, was streaked with gray.

Fargo grunted. Priests and ministers had been trying to convert the Indians for years. Not just the Nez Perce, but every tribe on the frontier. Men of the cloth had even gone to the Blackfeet, those implacable haters of white ways, and managed to convert some. When Fargo heard that, he couldn't believe it. "The missionaries were friends to the Nez Perce. I am a friend, too," he tried again.

"You not missionary."

"The Crows call me He Who Walks Many Trails," Fargo said. "I am their friend." He mentioned the Crows for a reason; they were on good terms with the Nez Perce, and the two often visited one another.

The old warrior touched his chest. "I be Wilupup Hemeen."

"Winter Wolf?" Fargo translated.

"We take you our village. Sit in council. Could be you live. Could be you not live."

Fargo had to submit to being hauled to his feet and swung onto the Ovaro. Winter Wolf took the reins and climbed on his Appaloosa. The other warriors followed.

"Mind if we talk?"

"Talk when at village."

Fargo sighed. He'd met a few Nez Perce in his travels. He hoped he would run across one of them when they got there. "There was a time when the Nez Perce treated whites as brothers."

Winter Wolf glanced back. "You not listen."

"I don't want your people to make a mistake," Fargo

said. "Harm me and the bluecoats will come. There will be war between the Nez Perce and the white man." He was exaggerating. It was unlikely the United States government would go to that extreme over the death of one man.

"We maybe take warpath anyway," Winter Wolf said. "All whites like you. They not listen. We tell stay away. But more whites come. And more and more and more."

"After gold. Yes, I know all about it. But I'm not in your land for that reason."

"All whites hungry for yellow rock," Winter Wolf said gruffly. "They try take our land. We not let them."

"I don't blame you. I would fight the whites, too, if I was a Nez Perce. But only the whites who were after gold."

To his surprise, Winter Wolf chuckled. "You think I dumb but I not dumb."

"I never said any such thing."

"How I know you not after gold? How I know you not speak with two tongues?"

"I could be lying, yes," Fargo admitted. "You have to take my word that I'm not."

Winter Wolf chuckled again. "Take word of a white man? You, how you say, funny."

The old warrior fell silent. Fargo tried to draw him out but Winter Wolf had apparently said all he was going to. They rode along until about sunset when they came to a small clearing near a stream. The warriors climbed down and two of the younger ones none too gently pulled him from the saddle.

"We're camping for the night?" Fargo asked. He tried to sound as if it didn't mean anything to him, when in fact the prospect of escape was being handed to him on a double-edged platter.

"We reach village in three sleeps," Winter Wolf disclosed.

Fargo was thrown onto his side next to the fire a warrior was kindling. Rising on an elbow, he saw two of the younger ones go off into the trees with their bows to

19

hunt. That whittled the odds but he wasn't about to do anything in broad daylight. Patience was called for.

The hunters returned with a doe, which was promptly butchered. The Nez Perce roasted their meat but they weren't finicky about how well done it was. Fargo's mouth watered and his belly growled but no one offered a piece to him. Finally he said, "My belly is empty. I sure could use some of that venison."

His mouth dripping, Winter Wolf said, "Good for you not eat. Maybe you listen better."

"Is this what you call Nez Perce hospitality?"

"It what I call smart," Winter Wolf said, and laughed.

Fargo sank onto his side and closed his eyes. He wanted them to think he was resigned to his fate. He listened to them talk, catching snatches of words here and there, enough to glean that the Nez Perce were on the brink of open hostilities with the whites. There had been clashes between gold seekers and warriors, and blood was spilled.

A young warrior made a comment to the effect that the gold hunters weren't the only ones the Nez Perce had to be concerned about. Some whites wanted to till the soil and build wooden lodges, as the warrior called cabins. The Nez Perce weren't going to allow that, either.

Fargo immediately thought of the wagon train. Sooner or later the Nez Perce were bound to come across it. Then again, the tribe laid claim to a large territory encompassing thousands of square miles, and they couldn't be everywhere at once. It was entirely possible Winston's bunch would have their cabins built before the Nez Perce discovered them. Either way, the outcome wasn't in doubt. The farmers would be wiped out.

A sliver of moon had been up several hours when Winter Wolf and his companions turned in. But first Winter Wolf came over and checked that Fargo's wrists were still tied. He also bound Fargo's ankles.

Fargo had a few anxious moments as Winter Wolf looped the rope around his boots. But the old warrior didn't think to slip a hand inside them to check for hidden weapons. Fargo's Arkansas stayed snug in its sheath. "I'm sorry we can't be friends," he remarked.

Winter Wolf had stood and turned but he stopped. "You white. I red. White and red fight. White and red kill."

"It doesn't have to be that way."

Sadness crept into the old warrior's features. "It not how I want. It how things be." He went to the other side of the fire and lay down to sleep.

Fargo made himself comfortable. It would be a while before all five drifted off. He was mildly surprised they didn't have someone stand guard, but then they were deep in their own territory, and he was tied.

Fargo had no desire to harm them. He wasn't their enemy. He wasn't an Indian hater, as so many whites were. But he couldn't go to their village, either. Hotter heads might prevail, in which case he could well find himself staked out over an anthill or skinned alive.

By midnight, heavy breathing and the lack of movement told Fargo the warriors were asleep. Slowly bending his legs back and up as high as they would go, he slid his boots toward his hands. When one of the younger warriors stirred, he stopped. He would only get this one chance. He mustn't make a mistake. Lives depended on him.

In the distance a wolf howled. One of the horses pricked its ears but thankfully didn't whinny or stomp.

Fargo tugged at his pant leg. The rope was so tight, he couldn't work his pants free. The irony brought a grim smile. It was his own rope, or a piece of it. He tugged harder, then pried at the knot with his fingernails. But Winter Wolf had done a good job. It took Fargo a quarter of an hour before the knot began to come undone. Another five minutes and he had it. He was so annoyed it took so long, he went to throw the rope but caught himself.

The warriors still slept.

Hiking his pant leg, Fargo slipped his fingers inside

his boot and palmed the Arkansas toothpick. Carefully sliding it out, he reserved his grip and sliced at the rope binding his wrists. The knife made all the difference. In seconds the severed rope lay on the ground.

Quietly unfurling into a crouch, Fargo moved toward the young warrior who had helped himself to the Colt. The warrior had been holding it when he fell asleep but now it lay next to his limp fingers.

Easing forward, Fargo reclaimed the six-shooter and holstered it. He could kill them. He could kill all of them as easy as could be. Five swift shots and they would no longer pose a threat to anyone. But Fargo didn't shoot. He killed only when he had to.

All Fargo needed now was his Henry. It was beside Winter Wolf. The old warrior had taken a fancy to the shiny brass receiver; all afternoon he had fondled the smooth metal. Fargo imagined how upset he would be when he woke up and found it gone, and grinned.

Rearmed, Fargo crept toward the horses. The Ovaro raised its head, waiting. Fortunately, the Nez Perce hadn't bothered to strip the saddle and saddle blanket. They had opened his saddlebags but left the saddlebags tied on. Right neighborly of them, Fargo thought.

The Appaloosas were curious about what he was up to and were watching him much as they would a mountain lion—with distinct unease. Fargo whispered to them, saying a few Nez Perce words, but stopped when one of the warriors mumbled in his sleep and rolled over.

Fargo waited to be sure the man was asleep. Then he quickly replaced the toothpick in his ankle sheath and slid the Henry into the saddle scabbard. He gripped the saddle horn and went to slide his toe into the stirrup. A few more seconds and he would be gone.

A yip rent the night. Not the cry of a coyote or wolf, but of the warrior named Winter Wolf. He had sat up and was groping for the rifle Fargo had taken. In his own tongue he shouted, "The white-eye! Stop him!"

Fargo swung onto the Ovaro. Moccasins pattered, and strong hands grabbed his leg. He kicked out, was rewarded with a cry of pain, and used his spurs to bring the Ovaro to a trot. An arrow whizzed over his shoulder, missing him by a whisker.

"After him!" Winter Wolf shouted.

Fargo wished he had spooked their mounts. But they couldn't see any better in the dark than he could, so he stood a good chance of getting away. Provided he didn't ride into a tree or a boulder. Reining sharply, he bent low in case more arrows arced his way.

The warriors were yelling. Apparently one of their horses was giving them trouble.

Fargo rode hard until the sounds faded, then slowed to a walk. There was no point in riding the Ovaro into the ground. When he finally drew rein an hour later, he was convinced he had lost Winter Wolf and his friends. Dismounting, he moved under a pine, wrapped the reins around a low limb, and sat with his back to the bole. He could use some rest.

Pulling his hat down over his eyes, Fargo willed his taut body to relax. It took a while but eventually he felt himself slipping away. He was on the verge of falling asleep when a rustling sound brought a whinny from the Ovaro and brought him to his feet with his Colt in hand.

It took a few seconds for Fargo to make sense of what he was seeing.

A dozen yards away something had stepped out of the trees. A huge, hulking shape, an animal breathing so heavily each breath was as loud as a blacksmith's bellows.

Fargo reached up to unwrap the reins from the limb, hoping the thing wouldn't attack if he tried to leave.

It growled. A growl so deep and so loud, only one animal could be responsible: a bear.

Fargo froze. He was furious at himself for letting it get so close without hearing it.

Bears were formidable brutes. They could easily tear a man limb from limb. Or rip a horse apart.

Fargo glanced at the saddle scabbard, at the Henry he should have shucked before he sat down to sleep. He was getting careless, and in the wild, careless was the same as a death wish. Steeling himself, he started to unwind the reins so he could get the hell out of there.

The bear rose onto its hind legs.

At first Fargo had thought it was a grizzly, but now he wasn't so sure. If it was a black bear, he might be all right. Black bears rarely attacked people. Then a second, smaller form came scampering around the big one, and his blood chilled. "Oh, hell."

It was a cub.

4

Mother bears were protective of their young. They attacked anything that came near their offspring. Anyone who stumbled on a cub was well advised to hasten elsewhere before the mother noticed or risk being torn to pieces.

The last thing Fargo wanted was a clash with a bear. It would take but an instant for him to jump up, grab a low limb, and climb into the pine. Once he was high enough, the she-bear wouldn't be able to reach him. But that meant deserting the Ovaro. He would as soon slit his wrists.

So Fargo went on unwrapping the reins while keeping his eyes on the mother bruin and the smaller version of herself. Both stood there and returned his stare. The reins came loose. Girding himself, Fargo slid the Colt into its holster, then launched himself at the saddle. He grabbed the saddle horn and swung his leg up and over.

The cub squalled.

The mother roared.

And Fargo got the hell out of there.

The Ovaro did not need goading. The smell of the bears was enough to make the stallion want to bolt. It wheeled around the pine and raced into the dark.

The mother bear gave chase.

Hunched low, Fargo slapped his legs and urged the Ovaro to greater effort. A raking paw nearly caught its flank. But just as he wouldn't desert the Ovaro, the mother bear wouldn't desert her cub. She pursued them only a short way and stopped. Venting her temper with another roar, she turned back to her ursine pride and joy.

Fargo let out a long breath. There was seldom a dull day in the wild, and this one had more than its share of excitement. First the wagon train, then the Nez Perce, and now this. "Things are supposed to come in threes but this is plumb ridiculous," he said out loud.

Half a mile of hard riding was enough. Fargo slowed, pushed his hat back on his head, and patted the Ovaro. "If I ever get old enough for a rocking chair, I'll put you out to pasture with two or three mares."

Some folks would say it was silly to talk to a horse. But they never spent day after day, month after month, year in and year out, with a horse as their only companion. After a while a man got to think of the horse as more than just an animal.

The night wind had grown brisk. It brought with it the cries of the creatures that preferred the night over the day: the howls of wolves, the yips of coyotes, the occasional bark of a fox, the hoots of owls. Once a mountain lion screamed. And from afar came the roar of the mother bear. To most those sounds spelled terror and made for a sleepless night. To Fargo they were as ordinary as grass.

About two hours of night were left when Fargo reined up. He needed sleep, and the Ovaro could certainly use more rest. This time he rode in among a cluster of large boulders, where they were less apt to be seen or scented, and curled up on his side in the dirt, his arm for a pillow. Hardly the most comfortable of beds but within seconds he was asleep and this time he stayed asleep until the squawk of a jay brought him around to greet the new day.

A hint of gold splashed the eastern horizon. Dawn was about to break. Fargo sat up, yawned, and stretched. He was stiff and sore and hungry. Rising, he opened his saddlebags and took out a bundle wrapped in rabbit skin. Inside was pemmican. A Cheyenne woman of his acquaintance had kindly given the pemmican to him. He chewed with relish. After he ate his fill, he replaced the rest and forked leather.

Unerringly, Fargo headed for the wagon train. He had a good idea of how far the wagons had traveled after he left them, and when he reached the spot where he thought they should be, there they were, strung out as before, canvas-backed tortoises on wheels. Caution bid him stop while he was still in the trees, and it was well he did.

Rinson, Slag and Perkins flanked the wagons. So did others Fargo hadn't seen before. He counted nine out-riders, all told. In the lead was a man with hair as white as snow, dressed in clothes more fitting for the streets of St. Louis or New Orleans.

Fargo shadowed them a while. All appeared peaceful. The farmers and their families chatted and laughed and now and then one of the young girls would break into song. Toward midmorning the white-haired man raised an arm and called a halt so they could rest their teams.

Fargo chose that moment to make himself known. As soon as he broke from cover, the white-haired man trot-ted to intercept him, bringing Rinson, Slag and Perkins along.

Drawing rein, Fargo leaned on his saddle horn. "You must be Victor Gore."

"That I am, sir. That I am."

Since all the others were unwashed and unkempt, Fargo figured their leader would be the same. But Gore was the opposite. The man's suit was clean save for the dust of the trail, and his white hair, mustache and short beard were neatly trimmed. Fact was, Victor Gore looked more like a parson than a wagon train pilot. Even more surprising, he wasn't wearing a revolver that Fargo could see.

"And you must be the scout my men told me about. Mr. Fargo, I believe it is?"

"That's me."

"I want to thank you for what you've done, sir," Vic-tor Gore said.

"How's that again?"

"You went to find the Nez Perce my men saw. To ensure they aren't a threat to the settlers, I'd warrant. I'm grateful."

Fargo cocked his head. This wasn't what he expected. This wasn't what he expected at all.

"Did you find them?" Victor Gore asked.

"It was a small hunting party," Fargo informed him. "They don't know about the wagons."

Gore beamed in relief. "That's good news, sir. Good news, indeed. These settlers are my responsibility, and I would be remiss if I were to let anything happen to them."

The man could talk rings around a tree, Fargo reflected. "How is it you're guiding this bunch? You don't strike me as the kind to do this for a living."

"I'm not. I've been in this part of the country before, though, back in my beaver days."

"You were a trapper?"

Gore nodded. "Pretty near twenty years ago, yes. I came west with a fur brigade and spent an entire fall, winter and spring in this very area, laying traps and collecting plews." He sighed wistfully. "Those were the days. I was young and carefree and thought the world was my oyster. The folly of youth, eh?"

"You don't look much like a trapper now," Fargo remarked.

Gore touched a hand to his suit. "You mean this? I shed my buckskins when I went back East. For the past dozen years or so I've lived in St. Louis, making my living as a merchant."

"Why leave that to come back here?"

Motioning at the majestic peaks, Gore said sentimentally, "This country gets into your blood. I've never stopped thinking about my beaver days, and I got it into my head that I'd like to see my old haunts once more before I pass on."

"You don't say."

"I got as far as Fort Bridger and learned of the difficulties with the Nez Perce. That's where I hired Mr. Rinson and his friends as my protection, you might say. It's also where I ran into Mr. Winston and his people."

"He mentioned that."

"Mr. Winston told me they were bound for Oregon, and went on and on about how wonderful it is there. I happened to mention that I knew of a valley every bit as fine, from my trapping days. That made him curious. He pestered me with questions, then called his people together and they decided they would like to see the valley for themselves. They asked if I would take them there, and here we are."

Fargo considered it possible, just possible, that Gore was telling the truth. A lot of people fell in love with the Rockies. He knew of half a dozen trappers who had gone east after the beaver trade died but missed the mountains so much, they came back. Others never left. The mountains were their home. Some took Indian wives and adopted Indians ways.

"I know what you're thinking," Victor Gore said.

"You do?"

"That it's most unwise of me to bring these people here, what with the current state of affairs with the Nez Perce."

"I was thinking that, yes," Fargo confessed.

"I tried to talk them out of it. I explained to Mr. Winston that the Nez Perce are upset over white incursions into their land. But he wouldn't listen. He insisted he can make friends with them, and he said that if I didn't bring him and his people, they would search for the valley themselves."

Fargo frowned. Winston hadn't told him that. "The damned fool."

"So you can see I'm not entirely to blame. I hope to sneak them in without the Nez Perce noticing. After that, they are on their own. I've made it clear their fate is on their shoulders, not mine."

"Tell me something." Fargo had decided to come right out with it. "Have you ever run into a family by the name of O'Flynn?"

Gore seemed genuinely puzzled. "The who? They're not with Winston, are they?"

"No. They came west about three months ago and vanished. They were last seen at Fort Bridger. The father of the wife hired me to find them."

"Oh. I was still in St. Louis then. Maybe they went on to Oregon or California and just haven't written to him. Or perhaps they decided to settle somewhere along the way, like Winston and his people are doing."

Both were possible, Fargo supposed. The sutler at Fort Bridger had told him a family that sounded like the O'Flynns had made it that far. Where they went after they left, the sutler couldn't say.

"I guess you'll be on your way now," Victor Gore said. "But you're welcome to stay for supper if you'd like, as a token of my appreciation for you helping us."

After what Fargo had overheard Perkins and Slag saying, he intended to hang around longer than that. But he nodded and said, "I'd be obliged."

The others weren't happy about it. Rinson shot him a dark glance. Slag scowled. Perkins fingered the hilt of his knife.

"Come join us," Victor Gore requested, and reined his dun toward the covered wagons.

Fargo gigged the Ovaro up next to the dun. "If you want, I'll try to talk the farmers into going on to Oregon."

"That would be wonderful. Lord knows, I've tried. But they're determined to settle the Payette River Valley." Gore shook his head. "People can be so stubborn."

Rachel was in the back of the wagon, and she smiled as Fargo rode past. He touched his hat brim to her and she did what he expected: she blushed.

Lester Winston and most of the other farmers came to meet him. Fargo told them about the hunting party.

He left out the part about being captured and bound, and the part about the mother bear.

"So you see?" Victor Gore said. "All is well. Now why don't we get under way? We can cover a lot more ground before dark."

Fargo made it a point to ride alongside the Winston wagon. "Is it true what Gore told me?" he asked Lester.

"About what?"

"That he tried to talk you out of going to the Payette River Valley?"

Lester's eyebrows puckered. "You must not have heard right. Didn't I tell you? Mr. Gore was the one who told us about the valley. It was his idea we go there. And I have to say, after hearing how fertile the soil is, and how much game is about, I agree with him."

"I wanted to be sure," Fargo said.

"Some of my people didn't like the idea. They were all for going on to Oregon. But Mr. Gore persuaded them to change their minds."

"A wonderful man," Fargo said. And a marvelous liar.

"He's got a silver tongue, that Mr. Gore," Lester declared. "My wife swears he could talk a patent medicine man into buying his own tonic."

Fargo agreed. It was the first thing that had struck him about Gore.

"I happen to like him," Lester had gone on. "If this valley turns out to be everything he claimed, he'll have saved us weeks of travel and I'll be forever in his debt."

"You don't think he could be lying?"

"To what end?" the big farmer demanded. "What purpose would it serve, him luring us off to the middle of nowhere? We hardly have any money and little else of value save our possessions and our wagons. I can't see anyone doing us harm over that. It's not worth the bother."

Lester had a point, Fargo reflected. But if Gore wasn't out to rob them, what *was* he up to?

Toward sunset another halt was called, and Fargo had

to hand it to Gore's men. They knew their business. They formed the wagons into a circle, gathered the horses and the teams and placed them under guard, and sent two men into the woods after firewood and two more out after something for supper. The farmers gathered in the circle while their womenfolk broke out pots and pans and whatnot.

Fargo brought the Ovaro into the circle. He was loosening the cinch when a shadow fell across him.

"What do you think you're doing?" Slag demanded.

"What does it look like?" Fargo replied. "I'm not going to leave the saddle on all night."

"I didn't mean that, stupid." Slag took a step and smacked the Ovaro. "No animals are allowed in the circle. We don't want their droppings all over the place. Take him and put him with the rest."

"No."

"I wasn't asking. It's a rule. The plow-pushers abide by it, and so do we. I'll take him myself if you won't."

"I wouldn't do that if I were you."

Slag gripped the reins, and smirked. "Oh? Why not? What do you aim to do about it?"

"Just this," Fargo said, and slugged him.

5

On the frontier, men were touchy about their horses. To steal one was an invitation for the thief to be guest of honor at a hemp social. Many a horse thief had died gurgling at the end of a rope. Even laying hands on another man's horse was frowned on. The same as laying a hand on another man's gun. Or, the supreme insult, laying hands on another man's woman.

Slag should have known not to try to take the Ovaro.

Fargo's fist caught him flush on the jaw and sent him tottering back. But Slag didn't go down. He swayed, shook his head to clear it, then set himself and did the last thing anyone would expect—he grinned.

"Not bad."

Fargo knew a brawler when he saw one. But he refused to back down. "I'm keeping my horse with me."

"Like hell you are." Slag balled his big fists and rapped his knuckles together. "After I pound you into the dirt, I'm adding him to the night herd."

"Like hell you are," Fargo mimicked him.

Raising his fists, Slag started toward him. "I've yet to meet the man I can't lick."

"There's always a first time," Fargo said, and then there was no time for anything as Slag waded into him. Fargo blocked, ducked, backpedaled, taking Slag's measure and finding that Slag was as good as his boast. Slag's arms were like the pistons on a steam engine. And God, the man was strong! When Fargo blocked, he felt it to his marrow. Under those dirty clothes, Slag was all muscle.

Fargo was no weakling, himself. His own sinews had

been sculpted to whipcord toughness by his years in the wild. He ducked under a jab and unleashed an uppercut that caught Slag on the jaw. For most men that was enough to bring them down. But all Slag did was stagger a couple of steps and shake his head again.

"You can do that all night and it won't hurt me much. I have a cast-iron chin."

"An iron head, too."

Slag took the insult as a compliment. "I've been beat on by three or four men at once and hardly felt it. Now what say I end this so I can eat my supper?"

And with that, Slag became a whirlwind. It was all Fargo could do to ward off the blows. As it was, some got through. He gritted his teeth and took the punishment, and gave as good as he got. He was dimly aware that others had gathered, and he heard the hubbub of voices. Someone shouted for them to stop—it sounded like Victor Gore—but if Slag heard, he paid no attention. Slag had his mind set on one thing and one thing only: pounding Fargo to a pulp.

Fargo circled, feinted, flicked a forearm to deflect a punch. He answered with a swift jab to the cheek that snapped Slag's head back but otherwise had no more effect than the jab of a feather.

Slag's brow furrowed. He seemed puzzled by something. Suddenly stepping back, he said, "No one has ever lasted as long as you have, mister."

"You haven't seen anything yet."

A looping swing nearly took Fargo's head off. He planted his left in Slag's gut, but it was like punching a board. He followed with a right cross that Slag blocked.

They were too evenly matched, Fargo realized. The fight could go on a good long while yet unless one of them made a mistake. In order to end it quickly, he suddenly dropped his arms and dove at Slag's legs. His intent was to bowl Slag over, straddle his chest, and punch him senseless. But slamming into those legs was akin to slamming into a pair of tree trunks. Fargo didn't knock him down. Worse, when Fargo quickly wrapped his arms around Slag's legs and sought to wrench them out from under him, Slag bent and clamped his hands on Fargo's neck.

"Now I've got you."

It was like having his neck in a vise. Fargo pulled and pried and hit Slag's forearms but the vise tightened and he was lifted bodily off the ground. Slowly but surely, he was being throttled to death.

Slag leered, confident he had won. He gouged his thumbs in deeper, saying, "How does it feel to die?"

Fargo drove his knee up and in.

It caused Slag to stagger and gurgle and turn near purple. His grip slackened. "That was dirty."

So is this, Fargo thought, and drove a finger into Slag's eye.

Slag howled and let go. He stepped back, pressing a hand to his eye. "Damn your bones!" he roared.

Tucking at the knees, Fargo swept his fist up from down near his boots and buried it in the pit of Slag's stomach.

Breath whooshed from Slag's lungs and he doubled over. Between his groin and his eye and his gut, he was in no shape to prevent the next blow from landing.

Fargo drew back his arm. He was set to end it.

Suddenly Lester Winston stepped between them and pushed against Fargo's chest. "Enough! We won't have this sort of thing, do you hear? You're upsetting the women and children."

Fargo almost hit him. Slowly lowering his arm, he looked around, and sure enough, many of the women were aghast at the violence and several small children clung to their mothers' legs in horror.

Winston wagged a thick finger. "Honestly. What were you thinking? I saw that you started it."

"My horse stays with me," Fargo said.

Victor Gore was only a few feet away, flanked by Rinson and Perkins. "Is that what this was about?"

Fargo unclenched his fists. His knuckles were sore and skinned, and his fingers hurt. "Your man wouldn't take no for an answer."

"He was only doing as he's been told," Gore said. "I'm beginning to regret inviting you to eat with us. But if you give me your word there will be no more of this petty behavior, you can stay."

"My horse stays with me," Fargo said again.

"Yes, yes, we've got that. I'm willing to make an exception. But don't test my good nature further."

A couple of Gore's men were helping Slag to stand. He angrily shook them off and glared at Fargo. "This isn't over, mister. No one does to me what you just did."

Gore shook his head. "You'll drop it, do you hear? Too much is at stake for this nonsense."

Fargo wondered what he meant by that.

"This is personal," Slag said. "You have no say."

Despite being a full head shorter and nowhere near as muscular, Victor Gore stepped up to Slag and put his hands on his hips. "Did I hear you right? Aren't you forgetting who's in charge, and why?"

"Damn you, Slag," Rinson said.

Slag wouldn't look Victor Gore in the face. Abruptly as meek as a lamb, he said quietly, "All right. I forgot. I'm sorry, Gore. I lost my temper when he hit me. It won't happen again."

"It better not."

Fargo was dumfounded. Slag wasn't the sort to back down to any man, yet here he was, cowed by a man twice his age, a man he could break as easily as he could snap a twig. Something was going on here, something more than met the eye. But what? he wondered.

Gore wheeled on him. "And you, sir. Do I have your word as well? Will you behave yourself?"

It galled Fargo to be treated like a ten-year-old. "I won't cause trouble if your men don't."

"Very well. Mr. Slag, to give you time to cool down, you will ride night herd the first two hours. Mr. Perkins will relieve you. The rest of you, go about your chores.

And Mrs. Winston, I hope you don't mind that I took the liberty of inviting Mr. Fargo to dine with us. Is that all right?"

"It's fine," the farmer's wife said, but she sounded dubious.

Fargo tied the Ovaro to a rear wheel of their wagon. As he did, a hint of lilac tingled his nose. He asked without turning, "Are you upset with me, too?"

"Not at all," Rachel said, stepping to one side. She had her hands clasped behind her back, which accented the swell of her bosom. "I thought you were magnificent."

Fargo chuckled. "I've been called a lot of things but never that." Leaning against the wheel, he let his gaze rove from her toes to her nose. "But now that you mention it, you're pretty magnificent yourself."

Predictably, Rachel blushed. "No, I'm not. I'm ordinary. And please don't look at me that way. You look as if you want to eat me alive."

"I do."

Rachel gasped and turned away, but turned right back again. "You make my ears burn."

"Just your ears?"

"Mr. Fargo, for a gentleman you are positively scandalous. My parents wouldn't approve."

"When did I ever claim to be a gentleman?" Fargo rejoined. "I'm a man and I like women. That's all there is to it."

"Oh, my. Surely you're not—" Rachel glanced about them, then lowered her voice. "Surely you're not suggesting what I think you're suggesting?"

"That I'd like to go for a walk with you tonight? That's exactly what is on my mind."

"You're too bold, sir."

"Are you going to stand there and tell me you haven't been with a man before? How old are you?"

"I'm twenty-two," Rachel said stiffly. "And whether I have or I haven't is none of your business."

"Which means you have. Do your folks know?"

Rachel's mouth dropped, but she quickly recovered her composure and leaned in so near she practically brushed him. "You might not be a gentleman, but I'm a lady and ladies don't discuss such things."

"I'm surprised you're not married yet, as good-looking as you are," Fargo said. Most women found themselves at the altar before they were twenty. Any later than that, and people started to whisper about spinsters and strange desires.

"Do you really think so?" Rachel touched her hair, then frowned and said, "Quit doing that."

"What?"

"Complimenting me. I'm trying to be mad at you and you make it very hard."

"Then we're even."

"How so?"

"When I look at you, part of me starts to feel hard, too."

Again Rachel gasped. Her eyes darted down, below his belt, and then up again. "That was crude."

Fargo laughed. "You looked, didn't you?"

"I don't know what to make of you. I honestly don't."

"I'll help you out," Fargo said. "I want to go for a walk and do things to you that will curl your toes. Was that gentlemanly enough?"

"You presume too much," Rachel said, but she didn't look away or blush, or leave.

"If I'm wrong, then don't go for a walk with me. But if I'm right, I'll meet you at the back of your wagon, say, about ten. It will be dark enough by then that we can slip away."

"Amazing," Rachel said. "You're too sure of yourself, by half. Women can't wait to rip your clothes off—is that how it goes?" She sniffed, and turned. "I need to help my mother. Don't expect to see me at ten."

Fargo watched her hips sway in exaggerated anger. "Things are looking up," he said to the Ovaro.

From under the covered wagon came a scraping noise. Squatting, Fargo found Billy about to crawl off. He grabbed hold of the back of the youngster's shirt and hauled him out. "I don't much like being spied on, boy."

"It's not my fault," Billy said defensively. "I was under there when you and Sissy came up."

"Then you heard everything?" Fargo could see him running to his parents, and his parents throwing a fit.

"So what if I did? I don't care what my sister does. Besides, as Ma keeps telling her, she's a grown woman and can do as she pleases."

"You're not mad at me?"

"For wanting to kiss my sister?" Billy laughed. "I was brought up on a farm, remember? I've seen cows do it. I've seen horses do it. Heck, I even saw two mallards in the pond do it. To me, you and Sissy are those ducks."

Fargo grinned. He had never been compared to a randy mallard before. "You have a good head on your shoulders, boy."

Billy laughed. "You don't fool me. You want me to be your friend so I won't tell Ma and Pa about your plans for tonight."

"Like I said, you have a good head on your shoulders."

"I also have empty pockets." Billy held out a hand. "A dollar will fill one of them just fine."

"You little outlaw."

"I could ask for two dollars."

Fargo snorted. "The most I'll give you is fifty cents."

Billy waggled his palm. "Didn't you say she's awful pretty? A dollar ain't much. And you have to promise to keep her out as late as you can."

"What for?"

"Sissy has some chocolate hid in the wagon. I've been trying to find it for weeks but she's never away from the wagon for very long."

Fargo fished a coin from his pocket, flipped it into the air and caught it, then dropped it in the boy's palm. "If I see your face on a wanted poster in a few years, it won't surprise me."

6

It had been a while since Fargo had home cooking, even if the cooking was done over a fire on the trail.

Martha Winston was a quiet woman. She didn't say a lot, and when she did, she said what was on her mind with no hemming and hawing. Lester was lucky in that she wasn't one of those women who talked a man to death. Doubly lucky, because she could cook. The food was delicious.

Supper consisted of thick venison steak, with salt if Fargo wanted some. Martha also heaped fried potatoes, cooked carrots and a couple of slices of bread smeared thick with butter on his plate. Saratoga chips were brought from the wagon and Fargo helped himself to a handful. For dessert there were cookies. She had made them days ago, and she didn't stint on the sugar. To wash it all down, Fargo was told to drink as much steaming hot coffee as he wanted. He downed six cups.

The meal alone almost made all that Fargo had gone through worth it.

After supper hour came the social hour. Other farmers and their wives came over to talk to the Winstons. Mainly they talked about farming, to where Fargo got tired of listening to whether this crop or that crop was better than this other crop or that other crop. And about growing seasons, and how much fertilizer should be used.

Rachel hardly said two words to him. She sat across the fire, her hands in her lap, and now and then gave him a furtive glance. He pretended not to notice except once when their eyes met. He smiled and she started to return it but caught herself.

Billy chattered like a chipmunk. He pestered Fargo with questions about being a scout and the army and Indians, and even asked how many men Fargo had killed. At that point, Martha cleared her throat and told the boy enough was enough, and he should hush. When Billy asked another question anyway, she reminded him that a hickory switch was in the wagon and he was never too old for her to tan his bottom. That shut him up.

Victor Gore ate with them but then went off to visit other families. It was pushing nine when he returned, and he wasn't alone. He brought Rinson along. Martha poured coffee for them and Gore made himself comfortable.

"I trust you enjoyed your meal, Mr. Fargo?"

"Never had better." Fargo noticed that Rinson sat to one side, his hand near his revolver.

"Good. Then you'll enjoy a good night's sleep and be well rested when you ride out in the morning."

"Who said I was?"

About to take a sip, Gore paused with the cup at his lips. "I beg your pardon?"

"Who said I was going anywhere? I might stick around a while. I'd like to see this Payette River Valley for myself."

Rinson shifted and scowled and looked at Victor Gore as if expecting him to say something, and Gore did.

"How is it you didn't mention this sooner?"

"What difference does it make?"

Gore drank and lowered his cup. "What possible interest would a man like you have in going there? You've been all over the West, I understand. You must have seen a thousand valleys."

"I'd like to be sure Lester and his friends get there," Fargo said. "What with the Nez Perce acting up and all."

The big farmer interrupted, saying, "That's awful kind of you. With your savvy of Indian ways, you can be of great help."

Victor Gore disagreed. "I know as much about Indians as any man. And we have enough guns to protect us, should it come to that." He smiled at Fargo. "I would much rather you went on your way. These people are under my care."

"No," Fargo said.

"Perhaps I haven't made myself clear. I'm in charge. Complete charge. It's one of the conditions I set and they agreed to before we left Fort Bridger."

Fargo returned the smile. "They agreed, not me. I can do as I please, and it pleases me to ride along a spell."

"I can have Mr. Rinson and his men prevent you from doing so."

"Not without losing a few, you can't. Maybe more than a few."

Gore lost some of his friendliness. "Are you threatening us?"

To Fargo's surprise, Martha Winston broke her quiet to ask, "Where's the harm if Mr. Fargo wants to come along? I don't know about you, Mr. Gore, but we're sociable folk. We enjoy the company of others."

"That's very neighborly of you, Mrs. Winston. In Ohio that's fine and dandy. Most folks are decent and law-abiding, like yourselves. But out here it's not like that. Out here renegades and killers are as thick as ticks. One must always be on their guard."

Now it was Lester who spoke on Fargo's behalf. "Surely you're not suggesting Mr. Fargo would harm us? I say he should be allowed to stay."

Victor Gore stalled by drinking more coffee. Rinson stared hard at him but Gore paid him no mind. Finally, Gore drained the cup, and sighed. "Very well. Never let it be said I'm unreasonable. Mr. Fargo can accompany us. But he must agree to abide by my decisions."

"You're in charge," Fargo said, and held in a grin.

"Yes, well. I think it only fair that I warn you. After what you did to Slag, my men don't think as highly of you as the Winstons do. You would be well advised not to cause any more trouble or they might take it into their heads to teach you a few manners."

"That would be something to see."

"I've seldom met a man so brimming with confidence," Victor Gore said. "And you know what they say. Too much of anything is never a good thing."

"There's another saying. Never stand too close to a snake or you might get bit."

"I've never heard that one."

Fargo had made it up. If the old trapper got the point, he hid it well.

But Rinson couldn't sit silent any longer. "I don't think it's right, him tagging along. We have enough to do without keeping an eye on him, too. And like you said, Slag and the others ain't happy about what he did."

"They will do as I tell them."

"You think too highly of yourself," Rinson said defiantly. "There is only so much we will abide."

Gore looked at him. "Is that a fact? In that case, you and anyone else who wants to can head back to Fort Bridger."

"Now hold on," Rinson quickly said.

"No. *You* hold on. Why must I keep repeating myself? I'm in charge. You'll do as I say or be gone at first light."

Rinson didn't strike Fargo as being a kitten but he meekly said, "I was only saying my piece. We'll do whatever you want. You hold the high card."

"And don't you forget it."

Fargo marveled at the control Victor Gore had over them. The old man bossed the cutthroats around as if they were his own personal army. "What high card would that be?" he inquired.

"I hired them, Mr. Fargo. They won't be paid if they don't do exactly as I say."

There had to be more to it than that, Fargo reflected. But Gore wasn't about to come right out and say it.

Just then someone produced a fiddle and began to play. Most of the farmers and their families gravitated toward the center of the circle, some clapping, some tapping their feet. A few linked arms and began to dance.

"I do believe I'll join in the festivities," Victor Gore said. Rising, he doffed his hat and took his leave, Rinson glued to his heels.

Martha Winston grasped her husband's hand. "Come. It will be nice to relax for a while."

Billy scooted off to join friends.

That left Fargo and Rachel. He looked at her and she pretended to be interested in her dress.

"Changed your mind about that walk?"

"Not on your life."

Grinning, Fargo rose. A sickle of moon hung low to the horizon and a multitude of stars sparkled like diamonds. "Suit yourself. I'm going for a walk." He went around the rear of the wagon and had barely taken six steps when she was at his side but staring straight ahead.

No one called out or tried to stop them. Most everyone was watching the fiddler and the dancers.

"I thought you weren't coming," Fargo said.

"Maybe a stroll would be nice, after all."

"It has to be your decision."

Rachel snickered. "First you invite me to traipse off into the dark with you, then you try to talk me out of it. And men say women are fickle."

The cool night air was a welcome relief from the heat of the day. Fargo pushed his hat back on his head and made for a stand of cottonwoods. From the mountains to the north wafted the ululating howl of a wolf. To the south, as if in answer, a coyote yipped. From the timbered slopes across the valley came the screech of an owl.

"Doesn't it ever scare you?" Rachel asked.

"What?"

"The wilds." Rachel swept an arm at the black well of the valley. "They sure scare me. Bears and mountain lions everywhere. Hostiles out to scalp every white they meet. I don't see how you stand it."

Fargo thought of his encounter with the mother bear. "It's not as bad as you make it out to be. Nine times out of ten a bear or a big cat will leave you be. And not all tribes are hostile. I could name half a dozen that have never harmed a white man."

"But there are many more that have," Rachel persisted. "I'm not a simpleton. I'm aware of the dangers.

I just couldn't go gallivanting all over as you do. It'll be bad enough settling in the Payette River Valley."

"I take it you wish you were back in Ohio."

"I never wanted to leave," Rachel said sadly. "It was Pa's idea, and he talked Ma into it. That didn't leave me much choice."

"Why didn't you stay in Ohio by yourself? You're a full-grown woman."

"I may be grown but I'm afraid I lack confidence," Rachel confessed. "Everyone says I'm so pretty but when I look in a mirror I see an ugly duckling."

Fargo stopped. Taking her arm, he turned her so she faced him. "You're as fine-looking as any filly I've ever met." He ran a finger over her silken hair and lightly brushed her ear.

"You're only saying that."

Fargo bent and looked her in the eyes. "May God strike me dead if I'm lying."

Rachel nervously giggled. "You shouldn't tempt the Almighty like that. My ma would call it blasphemy." Unexpectedly, she pressed her mouth to his in a quick, light kiss. A touch of her lips was all, and then she hastily pulled back.

"Aren't you the brazen tart," Fargo teased.

"You really think so?"

Even in the dark Fargo could tell she was blushing. "No. You're a lady through and through."

"Then what am I doing out here with you?"

"Even ladies get lonely." Fargo pulled her to him. She resisted, her body taut, but only until he molded his mouth to hers. Then, bit by gradual bit, she relaxed. Her tension drained away and she timidly raised her hands to his shoulders.

"You're awful good at this."

"What?"

"Don't play dumb. I don't mind. Really, I don't. There was someone else once, and he and I . . ." Rachel broke off. "Pa would have shot him for what we did, and Ma would have taken her hickory switch to me."

"They won't even notice we're gone."

"I hope not."

Fargo kissed her a second time, harder, and ran a hand from her shoulder down her spine to her hip. She shivered slightly, her breath fluttering into his mouth. He slid his tongue between her parted lips while at the same time he kneaded her thighs, first one and then the other. When he broke the kiss, her bosom was rising and falling as if each breath would be her last.

"Oh, my. That made me dizzy."

"Do you want to sit?"

"No, no. The farther we go, the safer it is."

Fargo led her into the stand. She clung to his arm, but whether from fear or passion, he couldn't say. A short way in he stopped and was about to kiss her when he gazed over her shoulder and thought he glimpsed movement between the cottonwoods and the covered wagons. His hand dropped to his Colt.

"What is it?" Rachel asked.

"I'm not sure." Fargo moved to the edge of the trees and she went with him, gluing herself to his side. When he stopped and crouched she did the same.

"See anyone?" Rachel anxiously whispered.

"No."

"I hope it's not my ma. She'll brand me a sinner and call down the wrath of the Lord on my head."

"Hush." Fargo looked and listened but the rustle of the cottonwoods was all he could hear over the fiddle and the voices. He let a couple of minutes go by, then said, "I reckon I was wrong."

"Maybe it was my brother. I wouldn't put it past him. He can be a brat at times."

If it did turn out to be Billy, Fargo reflected, he would demand his dollar back. He grasped her hand and began to rise, saying, "We're wasting time."

"Be gentle with me."

Fargo was about to say he would when something growled.

7

Instantly Fargo spun, his hand streaking to his Colt. It would be just his luck to run into another bear or some other predator. The night swarmed with them. But he didn't draw. Instead, he smothered a laugh.

Rachel Winston giggled.

A mother raccoon, her fur puffed up to make her more formidable, bared her teeth and hissed. Behind her were four young, born that spring from the looks of them.

Fargo had no desire to harm them. But a raccoon's teeth were sharp, and when a mother raccoon defended her young, she could be as fierce as a bear. "Shoo," he said.

Rachel did more giggling.

The young raccoons turned and scampered off. Still hissing, the mother backed away until she judged she had gone a safe distance. Then she wheeled and raced after her offspring, her bushy tail bobbing.

"Weren't they cute?" Rachel said. "We saw a lot of coons back home. They came to our pond to eat the frogs and fish."

Fargo was thankful it hadn't been something bigger.

"Do you think it was the coons you saw a minute ago?"

Fargo doubted it. How did they get behind him without him noticing? "Not likely," he said. Turning, he watched the grass a while, and when nothing appeared, he clasped Rachel's hand and led her deeper into the cottonwoods.

The wind rustled the leaves. Starlight made the pale boles gleam.

Fargo came to a clear spot and stopped. He went to kiss Rachel but she bowed her head.

"Have you changed your mind?"

"No, not at all. It's just that . . ." Rachel looked up and timidly smiled. "Give me a minute. I'm not a saloon girl. I'm not used to this, even if I have done it before."

"Take as long as you want," Fargo said, hoping it wouldn't be long at all.

"My ma would have a fit if she saw me."

"Oh, hell."

Rachel placed her hands on his chest. "I'm not backing out. Really I'm not. If I want to be with a man, I can. And you are just about the handsomest man I've ever met."

Fargo waited. She was talking to build up her courage. Some women did that.

"I'll remember this for the rest of my days. I want it to be just right. So please, don't be rough. Some men are rough and some women like that, I hear, but I'm not one of them. I don't like pain with my pleasure."

Fargo impatiently tapped his boot. Fortifying her courage was one thing; talking him to death was another.

Rachel tilted her head back and regarded the celestial canopy. "Isn't this romantic? You and me and the stars. It's like in a story or a poem."

If she started to recite poetry, Fargo was leaving.

With a shy grin, Rachel pecked him on the cheek. "I'm blathering, aren't I? Thank you for putting up with it. You are a gentleman at heart."

Fargo was no such thing but she could believe what she wanted. "Are you done or do you want to find flowers to pick?"

Rachel started to laugh, then caught herself. "Oh, my. When you're in the mood, you don't like being put off, do you?"

"I'm male," Fargo said.

"Thank goodness for that," Rachel responded, and

rising on her toes, she pressed her mouth to his. Her lips parted and the tip of her tongue delicately rimmed his lips. Suddenly pulling back, she grinned and impishly asked, "How was that?"

"It was a start."

"Your turn," Rachel teased.

Wrapping an arm around her slender waist, Fargo pulled her close. He kissed her hard and covered her right breast with his hand. She stiffened and gasped but slowly relaxed as he squeezed and kneaded. When he pinched her nipple through her dress, she uttered a low moan.

This time when they parted Rachel was breathing heavily and her voice was husky with craving.

"That was awful nice."

"It gets nicer."

They embraced again. His tongue and hers danced a velvet waltz. When he cupped both breasts at once, her breath turned to molten fire and she began to grind her hips against his.

Fargo was growing hot, himself. Hot and hard; his manhood was as rigid as steel. Her rubbing and her cooing and her soft, sweet mouth stoked his inner fire for long, pleasurable minutes, until finally he couldn't stand to stand there any longer. Suddenly dipping at the knees, he scooped her into his arms and carefully lowered her onto her back.

"Be gentle, remember?"

Fargo had half a mind to rip her dress off and ram into her like a bull elk in rut. But he slowly sank down and eased over her. They had an hour, he reckoned, before the settlers would start to turn in for the night and her parents would start looking for her. He might as well make the most of every minute.

The world receded. The night sounds dimmed. There was Fargo and the winsome woman under him and the trees around them and the grass they lay on, and that was all. Fargo explored her luscious body with his lips and his fingers, undoing buttons and stays where needed, and hiked the hem of her dress to get at her inner charms.

For Rachel's part, she wasn't content to lie there and have him do all the exploring. She pushed his shirt up and loosened his pants and lightly ran her fingers around his manhood.

Taking a gamble, Fargo grasped her hand and boldly placed it on his pole. She gasped again, and her whole body become as if carved from stone. For a few seconds Fargo thought he had gone too far. Then Rachel looked down and commenced to run her hand the entire length of his manhood.

"Goodness. It's so long and so hard."

Fargo had to cough to say, "It's supposed to be." It was all he could do to keep from exploding.

"Do you ever wonder why men and women are so different? I mean, why did God give women holes and men things to stick in them? And why is it women have big bosoms but men—"

Fargo shut her up with another kiss. He sucked on her lower lip. He ran his tongue from her chin to her ear and sucked and nipped her earlobe. Rachel was sensitive there. Squirming, she dug her fingernails into his shoulders. His hand found her knee and he ran his palm along her inner thigh, savoring the satiny feel. The higher his hand rose, the hotter her skin became. He pried at her undergarments and his fingers brushed crinkly hair. A quick flick, and his forefinger was in her moist sheath.

"Ohhhhh." Rachel threw back her head.

Fargo kissed her to silence her and she moaned into his mouth. He pumped his finger, causing her bottom to rise off the ground. Her legs widened and her ankles hooked behind his back.

The world receded even more. There was only pulsing pleasure that coursed through him as he aroused her to the heights of need. She cupped him, low down, and it was his turn to moan.

At last, the coupling. Fargo paced himself, rocking on his knees, each stroke as precise as a piston. He pumped and pumped and she thrust and thrust and they were panting into each other's ears when she cried out and spurted. Her release triggered his. He rammed into her hard until he was spent, then collapsed on her twin pillows.

Fargo was on the cusp of slumber when his sluggish senses flared to sharp life. For a few moments he lay still, trying to figure out what had snapped him out of the well of inner darkness. A rustling sound gave him warning. It didn't come from the trees above but from the nearby undergrowth. Rolling off Rachel, he started to pull himself together. He got his pants up and his belt hitched just as the vegetation parted, disgorging phantom forms. From the noise they made, and the way they moved, he could tell they weren't Nez Perce.

A few more steps and they were close enough for Fargo to identify. Anger welled, and he balled his fists as the foremost, the largest of the three, bent toward them.

Heaving upward, Fargo planted his fist on Slag's jaw. The blow rocked Slag onto his heels. The next moment Rinson sprang, seeking to grab Fargo's wrists. A boot to the gut dissuaded him. Then it was Perkins, flourishing his long-bladed knife.

"Not that!" Rinson barked. "Gore wouldn't want us to draw blood."

Perkins glanced at him and swore.

It was the opening Fargo needed. He unleashed a right cross that spun Perkins around and caused him to trip over his own feet.

Rachel chose that instant to sit up, blurting, "What in the world is going on?" She realized others were there, and covering her breasts, shrieked fit to burst their eardrums.

"Oh, hell," Rinson said.

Slag came in again, apparently determined to repay Fargo for earlier. His big fist swept at Fargo's face, but Fargo ducked and retaliated with a boot to the knee that sparked a roar of rage and sent Slag tottering.

Yells pierced the night from the direction of the covered wagons.

Perkins had firmed his grip on his knife and was hefting it as if of a mind to disobey Rinson and use it anyway.

Rinson was in a crouch.

Slag had steadied himself for another try.

Fargo discouraged all three by drawing his Colt. "I don't know what you peckerwoods are up to, but I'll damn well blow a hole in the next idiot who tries anything."

"I told you he was fast," Rinson said.

"I could have cut him if you'd let me," Perkins complained. "I could have gut him where he stood."

Rachel slid next to Fargo's legs and began frantically rearranging her clothes. "How dare you! What was the meaning of this?"

"You hush, girl," Rinson said.

"If you wanted it so bad, you should have told me," Perkins said, cupping himself. "I'd be glad to give you a poke."

Slag simply glared.

Judging by the racket, half the settlers were crashing through the undergrowth. A few more moments and the clearing was hemmed by farmers and their wives. Victor Gore was with them.

"What is the meaning of this? What was that scream we heard?" Lester Winston and his wife pushed through. At the sight of Rachel, both stopped in shock. Then Lester solicitously helped his daughter to stand, saying, "Are you all right? Was that you we heard?"

"I'm fine, Pa," Rachel declared. Now that she was dressed, she had regained her composure. Waving her hand at Rinson, Slag and Perkins, she said bitterly, "These three ruffians attacked Mr. Fargo."

"Attacked, hell," Rinson said. "We were defending your girl's honor." He turned to Victor Gore. "I noticed Fargo, here, was missing, so I asked around. One of the kids saw him and Miss Winston walk off together so we came looking for them."

"And found them here, doing I don't need to tell you what," Perkins related with lecherous glee.

Gore said harshly, "That will be enough."

"Didn't you hear me?" Perkins asked. "The scout and her came out here to fool around. I'm trying to be polite but if you want me to spell it out, I will."

"Enough," Victor Gore said again. "What the young lady does or doesn't do is her affair."

"Not if it makes trouble for us," Rinson broke in. "How can we protect them if they don't listen? You told them not to wander away from the wagons at night, and what did she do?"

"We can't force them to listen," Gore said.

Perkins swore. "I can't believe my ears. You're siding with them against us? When we were only doing what you told us to do?"

"To hell with this," Rinson said, and spun on a boot heel. "From now on these dirt-pushers can do as they please. I won't lift a finger to help them." He stalked off and Slag followed.

Perkins was bubbling like an overheated pan about to boil over. He stabbed a finger at Fargo. "This son of a bitch has a reckoning coming, and nothing you can say or do will change that." He stormed after his friends.

"I'm sorry," Victor Gore said to Lester. "Sometimes they forget they work for me. I'll give them a while to simmer down and talk to them again."

"I don't think they like us much," Lester said.

Martha was staring at Rachel, her arms crossed. "As for you, young lady, I can't say as I approve of your antics. Coming out here to be alone with a man you just met today. What will everyone think?"

"I don't care," Rachel said flatly. "I haven't done anything to be ashamed of."

"Is that the truth, daughter?"

"All we did was stroll about and admire the stars," Rachel fibbed. "Then those awful men attacked us."

"It won't happen again, miss," Victor Gore assured her.

"I hope not," Lester Winston said. "Not if they want the rest of their money. Our agreement was half in advance and half when we reach the Payette River Valley."

"I'm well aware of the terms we agreed on. And so far I've honored them, haven't I? This incident was regrettable. But my men were only trying to protect your daughter. If they were too zealous, I apologize."

If Fargo was any judge of character, Victor Gore was sincere. And if that was the case, then there was more going on than met the eye. Unraveling the mystery could take a while. The only thing was, Fargo didn't have a lot of time. In four days they would reach the Payette River Valley.

And then all hell might break loose.

8

Everyone was up an hour before sunrise. Hasty breakfasts were gobbled and washed down, in Fargo's case with four steaming cups of coffee. The teams were hitched, mounts were saddled, the children climbed into the wagon beds and the farmers and their wives perched on the front seats. Outriders were sent ahead and to the rear. Flankers moved off to either side. And then, at a shout from Victor Gore, the covered wagons lumbered northward, heading deeper into the dark heart of the wild.

Gore asked Fargo to ride with him.

Fargo didn't mind. He had been looking for an excuse to pump the man for more information about the Payette River Valley, and maybe glean a hint as to what Gore was really up to. But to Fargo's surprise, by the middle of the morning he was convinced the former trapper truly did come west again for one last glimpse of his old haunts.

Gore was quite the talker. He went on and on about his trapping days, about the streams he had worked and the plews he had raised. He mentioned how much he missed the annual rendezvous the trappers held.

"Yes, sir. Those were the days," Gore said fondly. "We were paid hundreds if not thousands for our peltries, and then spent most of it drinking and gambling and outfitting for the next season."

"You sound as if you would gladly live those times all over again," Fargo remarked.

"Would I ever! I was young. I was carefree. I lived

on the raw edge." Gore beamed. "Those were some of the best years of my life."

The heyday of the trappers was a little before Fargo's time. He had trapped on a few occasions, though, and sold a few mink and ermine pelts, among others.

"I remember it all so clearly," Gore went on in a dreamy tone. "How cold the water was when I set my traps. How heavy the beaver were when I pulled them out. What it was like skinning and curing the hides so they were just right and would earn top dollar. I remember everything."

"Did you regret having to give all that up?"

"I hated it so much, I was in a funk for half a year after I went back East. But a man has to make a living and beaver wasn't in fashion anymore. Damn silk all to hell, anyway."

Fargo chuckled. Silk hats had replaced beaver. But only until people switched yet again. The public was fickle that way. They were like butterflies flitting from flower to flower. Nothing held their interest for long.

"I envy you, sir," Gore unexpectedly said.

"In what way?"

"The life you live. I often wish I had bit the bullet and stayed. I might now be as you are. A scout. A frontiersman. Going where I please and doing what I will. Most men would give anything to live as you do."

"I never thought of it that way."

"Isn't that always how it is? We never appreciate the good things right in front of our faces. We're always looking at the next pasture and thinking it's greener than our own."

"I could never go back East to live," Fargo mentioned. "It would be like living in a cage. Always abiding by laws and rules." He never had liked being told what to do.

"You have more grit than I, sir. I freely admit it. I gave up the good life too easily."

After that Gore lapsed into silence.

Fargo thought about all he had learned. The important thing was that Gore's interest in the Payette River Valley seemed sincere, and his mention of it to the settlers at Fort Bridger appeared to be no more than happenstance.

Fargo let some time go by before he gnawed at the truth anew. "Rinson and his men," he said to strike up a new conversation. "I'm surprised a man like you would ride with them."

"They are a bit too zealous, aren't they?" Gore said. "But that's only because they take their job seriously. They don't want anything to happen to Mr. Winston and his people."

"You say that you never set eyes on any of them before you met them at Fort Bridger?"

Gore nodded. "Coincidence. Or the hand of providence, if you were to ask Mrs. Winston. I needed men and they were available."

"Lucky for you," Fargo said.

"If it hadn't been them, it would have been someone else."

Fargo shifted in the saddle. Rinson and Slag were off to one side. Both met his gaze with glares. "I'm not one of their favorite gents at the moment."

"I daresay you're not. I talked to Mr. Rinson last night after that little incident in the cottonwoods. He thinks you are a troublemaker and up to no good."

"Does he, now?"

"Yes, indeed. He suspects you are out to rob the farmers. So he and his men are keeping a close eye on you from here on out."

Fargo tried to look at it from Rinson's point of view. It was possible, just possible, that if Rinson was genuinely interested in protecting the settlers, he would think it suspicious of him to attach himself to the wagon train as he had done.

"I should tell you," Victor Gore said. "Mr. Winston and his people don't have much money. They spent most of what they had buying their wagons and outfitting for their journey."

"I'm not out to rob them."

"I hope not. You're terribly quick with that pistol of yours, and you punch as hard as any man I've ever seen, but Mr. Rinson and his men are tough, too. They won't hesitate to throw lead if they have to."

"I'll keep that in mind."

Gore swatted at a fly. "Rinson sure is clever. I never would have thought of offering myself as a protector."

"A what?"

"That's what he calls himself. There are plenty of pilots and guides and whatnot. But Mr. Rinson only hires out to protect wagon trains. So he calls himself and his friends protectors."

Fargo could see where a notion like that might catch on. Wagon trains were often beset by hostiles. Outlaws, wild beasts and other perils compounded the danger. Emigrants would gladly hire an outfit to see them safely through to Oregon or wherever else they were bound. "How much did Rinson ask for?"

"Money, you mean? His fee was two hundred dollars, half in advance, the other half when we reach our destination. Mr. Winston and his people pooled nearly all the funds they have left to pay him."

Fargo did the math in his head. If Rinson and his men divided the money equally, that came to twenty-five dollars each. Not a lot for putting their lives in peril. Then again, if a man was frugal and a little lucky at cards, he could spend a month or more at a saloon, drinking and taking up with doves. Some men would rate that worth the risk of taking an arrow. "Are the settlers paying you, too?"

"Goodness, no. I was going to the valley anyway. Mr. Winston offered to pay me but I wouldn't hear of it."

"You're doing this out of the goodness of your heart?"

A grin split Gore's face. "You needn't sound so sarcastic. I just told you I was going there anyway."

"Even though the Nez Perce are stirred up?"

"None of us live forever, Mr. Fargo."

When the sun was straight overhead Gore called a halt. The farmers gladly spilled from their wagons to stretch and stroll about. Some took the time to eat a quick meal.

Fargo was by himself, sitting under a pine with his back to the trunk and his hat brim low over his eyes, when a dress swished and a warm hand brushed his cheek.

"You haven't said ten words to me all morning."

Fargo pushed his hat back on his head and squinted up at Rachel Winston. "I'll make it up to you tonight."

Rachel grinned and sank down, her shapely legs coiled under her. "What do you have in mind, kind sir?"

"What do you think?" Fargo rejoined, and went to reach for her.

"Not in broad daylight!" Rachel cried, drawing back. "Everyone will talk."

"They're talking anyway."

"Yes. But they're doing it behind our backs. Were we to carry on now, some might see fit to complain to my ma and pa, and they're upset enough with me as it is."

"They don't approve?"

"What kind of question is that? Of course they don't approve. It would be different if we were to be married. As it is, they think I'm a woman of loose morals."

"They said that?"

"No, but I can read it in their faces. I've disappointed them, I'm afraid." Rachel leaned closer and lowered her voice. "But it was worth it. I wouldn't trade last night for anything. Maybe that makes me a hussy. If so, so be it."

"It's not as if you're going to go to work in a saloon or walk the streets at night."

"You're forgetting women have it harder than men. An unwed man can lie with a woman and no one says a word. They take it as natural. But let an unwed woman lie with a man and suddenly she's a trollop and of no-account. I ask you, is that fair?"

"No," Fargo admitted.

"Men are free to do as they please but women must walk around with chastity belts on."

Fargo laughed.

"It's not the least bit funny. Were it up to me, women would have the same freedom men do. Is that so wrong?"

"No," Fargo agreed again.

"Well then," Rachel said softly, "tonight, if you're willing, I'll make a hussy of myself. But we must be discreet. We can't let anyone see us leave, and we have to watch out for Rinson and his friends in case they come looking for us."

"They won't make that mistake twice," Fargo predicted.

"Don't put anything past them. I overheard Rinson and Slag talking. They resent you being here, for some reason. Slag is all for making you leave whether you want to go or not but Rinson told him it might make my pa or Mr. Gore mad. They must think my pa approves of you and me carrying on." Rachel tittered. "We'll let them go on thinking that if it keeps them off your back."

A shadow fell across them.

Fargo looked up, thinking it was her father or mother but it was Rinson, and he wasn't alone. Slag and Perkins were with him. "Speak of the devil."

Rinson held his hands out, palms up. "We're not looking for more trouble, mister. We came over to talk, is all."

"I'm listening."

Hooking his thumbs in his gun belt, Rinson forced an oily smile. "We want you to leave."

"Hell," Fargo said.

"Don't get riled," Rinson said quickly. "We're asking real nice. As a favor to these farmers, it would be best for everyone if you lit a shuck."

"How long before you get it through your heads? I'm sticking around a while."

Perkins said flatly, "You don't want to do that."

"No, you sure don't," Slag echoed.

"Why not?"

They swapped glances but said nothing.

"Get used to me," Fargo said.

Rinson sighed and lowered his arms. His hand was near his Remington but he made no move to draw it. "No one can say I didn't try. I asked real polite and you threw it in my face."

"Saying no was the biggest mistake you ever made," Perkins said.

"The biggest." Another echo from Slag.

"Go pester someone else," Fargo snapped.

Their expressions didn't bode well as the three so-called protectors turned and walked off.

"Why did they do that?" Rachel wondered. "My pa made it clear you can stay as long as you want."

All afternoon Fargo rode alongside the Winstons' wagon. He saw little of Vincent Gore, who went on ahead with Perkins and two others to find a spot to camp for the night.

The protectors stayed away from him. Whenever Fargo glanced at any of them, they made it a point to look away. That alone made him suspicious. They were trying too hard to make him think they were willing to leave him be.

Along about four dust rose to the north. Fargo figured it was Gore and he was right, but they were pushing their horses as if the animals couldn't go fast enough to suit them.

"We found a spot that would be perfect for our night camp," Gore announced after the settlers hastily gathered. "But a bunch of Nez Perce got there first. I counted eighteen, and they were wearing paint."

Fargo frowned. It was a war party, not a hunting party.

"Do you reckon they're searching for us?" a farmer anxiously asked.

"Lordy, I hope not," a woman said. "I don't want to spend the rest of my life in some buck's lodge."

"Enough of that kind of talk," Lester said.

"Stay calm," Victor Gore urged them. "I doubt the Nez Perce know we're here yet."

"But you can't be sure," someone remarked.

"There's one way to find out," Gore said. "We must send someone to spy on them and learn what they are up to."

"It will be awful dangerous," Lester said. "Who did you have in mind?"

Victor Gore's gaze drifted to Fargo, and everyone imitated him. "I was hoping for a volunteer."

"Hell," Skye Fargo said.

9

There were twenty-four, not eighteen.

The hoof prints told Fargo that much. They also told him the Nez Perce hadn't camped overnight at the clearing where Victor Gore told Fargo he had spotted them. The tracks led through the clearing and out the other side without stopping.

It raised a couple of questions in Fargo's mind. Why did Gore tell him the Nez Perce were camped there when they weren't? And what were the Nez Perce doing there to begin with? If they were painted for war, as Gore claimed, they were either planning to raid an enemy or coming back from a raid.

Either way, the tracks plainly pointed to the east. The wagon train was to the south. So the settlers were safe enough for the time being.

But now Fargo had a decision to make. He could ride back and tell Gore and Winston all was well or he could make certain all was well by following the war party a short way to be sure they didn't stay in the area.

Fargo swore and gigged the Ovaro to the east.

By then the sun was only a few degrees above the horizon. Sparrows chirped in the brush. Several deer watched him go by without showing any fear. A squirrel leaped from limb to limb high in the trees. All signs that the woods were peaceful. But Fargo wasn't fooled. The wilds were a fickle mistress—peaceful one moment, erupting into violence the next. He rode with his hand on his Colt. Every so often he rose in the stirrups to scan the terrain ahead.

The shadows lengthened. Soon the bright glare of day would give way to the spectral gray of twilight.

Fargo pondered as he rode. It bothered him that he couldn't figure out what Rinson and the other so-called protectors were up to, or how, exactly, Victor Gore fit into the scheme of things. Gore had talked the farmers into hiring Rinson but he might have felt he was doing the farmers a favor.

It bothered Fargo, too, that the farmers wouldn't listen to his advice and get the hell out of Nez Perce country while they still could. No valley, no matter how ideal, was worth the price the farmers would pay when the Nez Perce found out they were there.

Then there was Rachel. Fargo had taken a shine to the girl and didn't want her harmed. He had half a mind to throw her over his saddle and take her away by force when he left.

Engrossed in his musing, Fargo forgot to rise in the stirrups. He was jolted back into the real world when the Ovaro suddenly stopped of its own accord and pricked its ears.

Fargo looked up, and wanted to kick himself. He had nearly blundered onto the Nez Perce. Quickly reining into cover, he bent low over the saddle horn.

Mounted Nez Perce were winding through the woods. With a start, Fargo realized it wasn't the entire war party but only six warriors, and they were coming *toward* him, not moving away.

Fargo firmed his grip on the reins. He wondered if the six were looking for him, although he couldn't see how that could be. He had been careful not to cross open areas. And his Henry, with its shiny brass receiver that could flash in the sun and give him away, was snug in his saddle scabbard.

Gore had been right about one thing. The warriors, and their mounts, were painted for war. One horse bore the stick figure of a man to show its owner had ridden an enemy down in combat. Another had a crescent high on its front leg and the symbol for a bow on a rear leg to show that the warrior had fought in a battle at night.

The Nez Perce were casting about for sign, and four had arrows nocked to the sinew strings of their bows.

They were hunting, Fargo guessed. War parties had to eat. And if they kept coming they might spot the Ovaro's tracks and know by the pinto's shod hooves that a white man was nearby.

The tracks would lead them straight to him.

Fargo reined to the north and moved off at a walk. He stayed bent low and prayed none of the warriors would glance up and catch sight of him. But fate had other ideas. He covered less than a dozen yards when a sharp cry rang out.

A warrior with a bow was pointing at him.

"Damn it." Fargo jabbed his spurs and brought the Ovaro to a gallop. He had confidence in the stallion but Appaloosas were fine animals, too, with a lot more stamina than the grass-fed ponies of the plains tribes. He was in for a long chase.

The Nez Perce came on fast. An arrow whizzed past but that was the only shaft they wasted. He didn't resort to his Colt. Shots might bring more.

Fargo concentrated on increasing his lead but the warriors were determined to keep him in sight, and their Appaloosas were equal to the challenge. Half a mile of hard riding convinced him he must do something drastic.

A thicket sparked an idea.

Fargo raced around it. The moment he was on the other side he brought the Ovaro to a sliding stop next to it. Soon the Nez Perce came flying by on either side. They were intent on the woods ahead and went past without seeing him.

Halting on the reins, Fargo used his spurs again. Only *he* was now chasing *them*. They had lost sight of him and slowed, and were looking around in bewilderment.

As the Ovaro swiftly overtook the last warrior, Fargo unlimbered his Colt.

The warrior glanced over his shoulder, his face mirroring disbelief. It slowed his reaction.

Fargo slammed the Colt against the warrior's temple and sent him tumbling to the earth. Without slowing Fargo bore down on the next, a stocky warrior armed with a Sharps rifle. The warrior never got the chance to use it. Once again the Colt flashed. Once again the barrel struck flesh and bone. And once again a warrior pitched headlong from his warhorse.

Two down and four to go.

Fargo caught up to the third warrior and reined in close. The man shot a surprised glance at him and started to turn. Fargo hit him full in the face and cartilage crunched.

Three down now.

Of those remaining, one was to Fargo's left, the other two to his right. He reined to the left.

It had to happen. This warrior was more alert than the others. He glanced back and immediately yelled to warn his companions. Then he tried to bring his bow into play.

An extra burst of speed brought Fargo up close. He swung and hit the bow, and it went flying. The warrior clawed for a knife and was whipping it from its beaded sheath when the Colt caught him across the jaw. One blow wasn't enough. The warrior swayed but stayed on. A second blow remedied that.

The last pair had heard the yell and were streaking toward Fargo. Both held bows with shafts ready to fly.

Fargo had no choice. He snapped off a shot. The slug cored a warrior's shoulder and half twisted him around but he stayed on his horse. Then an arrow loosed by the last warrior buzzed within a whisker's width of Fargo's ear. Hugging the Ovaro, he sought to outdistance them, but they and their Appaloosas were as tenacious as always.

So far Fargo had not had to kill any of them. Nor did he want to. He had no quarrel with the Nez Perce. In the past, he'd made friends with a few, and if the truth be known, he didn't blame them for wanting to drive the whites out of their territory. He would do the same if he were a Nez Perce. The whites had no right to claim land the tribe had roamed for God knew how many generations.

When next Fargo looked back only one warrior was still after him. The man he shot in the shoulder had stopped.

By now the sun was dipping below the horizon. More shadow than light cloaked the woodland and it took all of Fargo's considerable skill as a horseman to thread the Ovaro through the trees safely. Unfortunately, the doggedly persistent warrior was also a good rider, and while he didn't gain, he didn't lose ground, either.

The stamina of their mounts would decide the outcome. Appaloosas were renowned for their endurance but the Ovaro was no swayback. The stallion could go strong for miles but it had already been through a lot and Fargo had a hunch it would tire before its pursuer. He decided on another reckless gamble. But he needed the right spot.

Presently his wish was granted. The forest thinned, giving way to broken country split by gullies and sprinkled with boulders. The Ovaro flew down the slope of a dry wash and up the other side, dust and stones spewing from under its flying hooves.

The Nez Perce gave voice to a war whoop. He had an arrow notched but was wisely saving it for when he was so close he couldn't miss.

A clutch of cabin-sized boulders reared in Fargo's path. He reined wide to go around, as he had done back at the thicket. And again as he had done at the thicket, when he came to the far side he reined in behind them. But only for the brief second it took to launch himself from the saddle, yank the Henry from the scabbard and swat the Ovaro on the rump.

The pinto kept going.

Fargo dashed to the edge of the boulders. Reversing his grip on the Henry, he set himself, ready to wield it as a club. There was a chance he might damage it, though, so when his foot bumped a rock as big as his fist, he suddenly changed his mind. Bending, he scooped up the rock. He hefted it a few times, then cocked his arm.

Hooves pounded, and around the boulder swept the Appaloosa. The warrior spied the riderless Ovaro up ahead, and stiffened.

That was when Fargo threw the rock with all his might.

The warrior reeled, blood pouring from a jagged gash on his forehead. He brought his mount to a halt, reined around, and raised his bow. But he couldn't let the arrow fly for all the blood in his eyes. Blinking and wiping his forearm across his face, he tried to sight down the shaft.

By then Fargo was on him. Seizing an ankle, he un-horsed the Nez Perce. The man landed on his shoulders and rolled to scramble to his feet but he was only half-way up when the stock of Fargo's rifle slammed against his head and he crumpled in a heap.

Fargo stepped back, ready to swing again if he had to, but the Nez Perce was unconscious.

Sticking two fingers into his mouth, Fargo gave out a piercing whistle that would bring the Ovaro back. The lathered Appaloosa had already stopped and was standing with its head down.

Fargo scoured his back trail for the others. None were in view but they soon might be. He must make himself scarce, and quickly. Hurrying to meet the Ovaro, he forked leather, and paused.

Fargo had a problem. He wanted to head straight for the wagon train but if he did, the Ovaro's tracks would lead the Nez Perce right to them. He must lose the war party before he could head back and that might take some doing.

The wagons were coming from the south. The war party was to the east. Fargo could go north but that was the direction the wagons were traveling. He could go west, too, but if the warriors lost his trail and headed to the east as they had been doing, they might cross the wagon train's trail.

Add to that the possibility that one or more of the six Fargo clashed with might go fetch the rest of the war party.

Fargo reined to the southeast. It would take him away from the wagon train and the settlers, but dangerously near the war party. Since it would be dark soon, he was confident the Nez Perce wouldn't be after him until daylight. He had all night to find a way to shake them.

In due course the sun sank and a few dim stars speckled the firmament. They brightened as the sky darkened and multiplied like ethereal rabbits.

Fargo found the Big Dipper. In the northern hemisphere, the two stars that made up the cup of the Dipper farthest from the handle always pointed at the North Star. Knowing where the North Star was enabled him to tell direction at night. Every frontiersman knew the trick.

Fargo's belly growled but he ignored it. Food would have to wait. Besides, hunger helped to keep a man awake and sharp, and he might need to ride all night.

The mountains came alive with savage cries and ululating howls. The meat eaters were abroad, a legion of fang and claw that feasted from dusk until dawn and then returned to their dens and burrows to sleep their lethargy away and greet the next night as ravenous as on the last. A cycle of hunger and blood, as old as time itself.

Fargo wasn't worried about the predators. A grizzly might take an interest in him but most everything else would give him a wide berth. The mere scent of a human was enough to cause most meat eaters to slink silently away.

Weariness nipped at Fargo's sinews. He had been on the go since before sunup. Between the hours in the saddle and his fight with the Nez Perce, he wouldn't mind a few hours rest. Stifling a yawn, he shrugged the tiredness off. Sleep, like food, had to wait.

A belt of woodland brought him to the base of a mountain. He rode along the bottom until he came to a stream. Reining into the center, he headed upstream. It was shallow but flowed swiftly enough that by morning all traces of the Ovaro's tracks might be obliterated.

"We can only hope," Fargo said out loud.

Another hour of riding brought him to a narrow gap. He passed through, the rock walls virtually rubbing the Ovaro's sides, and emerged to discover a range he had never visited before. He would love to explore it but it would have to wait. Swinging to the south, he rode in a wide circle that would eventually bring him back to the wagon train.

Fargo had a fair notion of where the train should be. He estimated it would take him two hours to reach it. He would try, yet again, to warn the settlers off. With the countryside swarming with Nez Perce, the farmers would be lucky to live long enough to plant seeds.

Then from out of the night came a sound other than the howls of wolves and the yips of coyotes.

It was a scream, torn from a human throat.

10

It came from the east, from out of the dark heart of the unknown range. Faint but unmistakable, it rose to a piercing shriek then gradually faded.

Fargo's skin prickled. That was a death cry if ever he heard one. He drew rein and briefly debated. Should he head west to the covered wagons or east into the unknown? He reined east.

It was like looking for the proverbial needle in a haystack. There was no light to guide him, not so much as a finger of campfire flame. He relied on his instincts to pinpoint the approximate area the scream came from.

The somber mountains gave way to a narrow valley so thickly chocked with timber that Fargo couldn't see ten feet. Wary as a cat in a room full of sleeping dogs, he went a quarter of a mile. Far enough, he thought, to show he must be mistaken. He was about to rein around when an acrid odor tingled his nose.

Smoke.

Fargo sniffed. He turned his head from right to left and back again. There could be no mistake. The smoke was drifting his way from deeper in the inky valley.

The clomp of the Ovaro's hooves were the only sounds. Although they were muffled by the carpet of pine needles, to Fargo they were thunderclaps that could be heard by hostile ears. He kept his hand on his Colt.

The acrid smoke scent grew stronger.

Up ahead a tiny red sprite flared, a flickering dervish that writhed and danced to the whispers of the wind.

A clearing spread before him.

Fargo came to a stop. At its center was the sprite, all that remained of a campfire. It didn't cast enough light to illuminate the vague shapes and figures that littered the ground around it.

A new odor struck Fargo. Another unmistakable smell. This time it was the scent of blood. Freshly spilled blood, and a lot of it. He waited, refusing to expose himself until he was sure it was safe. After several minutes of complete silence, he kneed the Ovaro. Ever so warily, he picked his way around the sprawled figures.

Dismounting, Fargo hunkered. He puffed on the flame and it grew, revealing a nearby pile of broken sticks. He added a few and blew on the smoldering embers and soon had a fire. A small fire, a fire that wouldn't be seen from any great distance.

It revealed a slaughter.

Five white men lay in the throes of violent death. One had his throat slit. Another had his head bashed in by a war club. A third had taken an arrow to the chest and another shaft low down in the ribs. Their end had been swift, the attack so sudden that they had not gotten off a shot. They had not been dead long. It was impossible to say which one had uttered the death scream Fargo had heard.

None had been scalped.

Their guns and knives had been taken. Packs had been torn open and the contents scattered about. Whatever did not interest their slayers had been left where it lay.

Picks and shovels and pans told Fargo what he had already guessed. The five were gold hounds. They had heard the rumors about gold in Nez Perce territory and snuck in to find it, and paid for their arrogance with the coin of their lives.

Ironically, Fargo found no proof the Nez Perce were responsible. No arrows had been left. No lances. There was nothing that would identify the killers. But this was their land and it was unlikely another tribe was to blame.

Fargo figured the attack took place about sunset, when the whites were settling in for the night and their guard was down. Believing them dead, the Nez Perce took what they wanted and rode off. But one man had lingered at death's door for hours, voicing that scream when he finally succumbed to the reaper.

Fargo wished Lester Winston and the other farmers could see this. Maybe it would convince them to turn back before it was too late. Before the Nez Perce discovered them and drenched the soil with more blood.

Since he had the fire going, Fargo made use of it. A coffeepot had been knocked over. He righted it and put fresh coffee on to brew. He needed some to stay awake and alert. The Nez Perce were gone, so there was little danger. He wondered if it was the same war party he had been trailing.

Surrounded by bodies, the pungent smell of blood in the air, Fargo cupped the hot tin cup in his hands and savored each swallow. Warmth spread from his stomach to his limbs.

Fargo was glad to relax for a bit. He leaned back and looked at the Ovaro and saw that the pinto was staring off up the valley. Swiveling, he did the same but dark baffled his efforts to penetrate it. He raised the cup to drink more coffee.

That was when, faint but clear, a horse whinnied.

In the bat of an eye Fargo was on his feet. He upended the cup as he dashed to the Ovaro. Swinging up, he reined around and flew into the forest.

Thirty yards was enough.

Fargo came to stop, took a moment to shove his cup into a saddlebag and palmed his Colt.

It was a good ten minutes before a mounted warrior came out of the trees on the far side of the clearing and stopped. Others joined him. Fifteen in all, their faces painted. The first warrior brought his Appaloosa up next to the fire. He regarded the flames with obvious puzzlement, then glanced at each of the bodies. Another warrior said something and the first one answered.

Fargo had been wrong. The Nez Perce hadn't left. They had gone up the valley and made camp. His rekindled fire had caught their eye and they had come to investigate.

The first warrior climbed down. He sank to one knee and lightly touched a finger to the coffeepot. Jerking it back, he stood and scanned the clearing, then said a few words that caused the rest to raise their bows and lances and begin to spread out.

"Damn it to hell," Fargo said under his breath. They knew someone must be close by.

Fargo moved off at a slow walk, twisting at the hips so he could keep one eye on the Nez Perce. Contrary to popular belief, Indians weren't cats. They couldn't see any better in the dark than white men. But their ears worked just as well, and the slightest sound would bring them in a rush.

So much for some coffee and some rest.

The minutes crawled on the scales of a slow snake. Fargo's every nerve jangled when the Ovaro stepped on a twig that crunched loudly. He was sure the warriors had heard, but they gave no sign that they did.

It took some doing but he made it to the end of the valley. Once around the mountain, he breathed easier.

The rest of the night proved uneventful.

A pink blush marked the eastern sky when Fargo at long last set eyes on the covered wagons. The camp was astir, the women making breakfast while the men prepared to get under way. Bone weary, he rode past a sentry, who didn't say a word, and into the circle.

The farmers gathered around, eager to hear what Fargo had to say. So did most of their self-styled protectors. He didn't make much of his escape but he did of the dead gold hunters, finishing with, "If you don't turn back, you could end up the same. You've been lucky so far but no one's luck holds forever."

"What you call luck," Lester Winston said, "we call the hand of providence. The Lord will watch over us."

"Those gold hounds probably thought the same," Fargo pointed out, but he was wasting his breath. The farmers were determined to get to the Payette River Valley, come what may.

Fargo needed sleep, needed sleep badly He mentioned it to Rachel who went and talked to her father, and Lester came over to offer Fargo the use of their wagon.

"You can tie your horse on the back. We have plenty of blankets and a quilt we spread out at night. Make yourself comfortable."

Fargo was grateful. The creak and rattle of the wagon bed didn't bother him a bit. Nor did the bouncing and the swaying. He drifted into a deep, dreamless sleep from which he didn't awaken until the middle of the afternoon. Poking his head out of the blankets, he blinked in the bright sunlight that streamed in under the canvas.

"About time you woke up, mister." Billy was sitting cross-legged, his elbows on his knees. "I'm tired of being a mouse."

Befuddled with sleep, Fargo had no idea what the boy was talking about. "A what?"

"Ma said I had to be as quiet as a little mouse while you were sleeping or she would have Pa take a switch to me."

"Oh." Fargo slowly sat up. They were alone. Rachel was on the front seat with her parents.

"They say you fought Indians yesterday. Is that true?"

"I ran more than I fought."

"But you did fight?" Billy grinned excitedly. "I can't wait until I'm old enough to tangle with some of those red devils."

"They're people, like us," Fargo said. He rubbed his chin, then jammed his hat back on.

"What kind of talk is that? Indians are savages. Everybody knows that. They kill whites every chance they get. My grandpa used to say that the only good redskin is a dead redskin."

"Your grandpa is a jackass."

Billy stiffened and balled his small fists. "Take that

75

back. No one talks about Gramps like that. He was the best man I ever knew." Billy paused. "He died a year ago. Came down sick with a cough and got worse and worse until one morning Ma sent me to wake him for breakfast and he wouldn't answer me or move or anything. He was dead."

"He was wrong about Indians."

"Mister, I liked you until now. I'm not stupid. Most Indians hate us and we hate them right back."

Fargo cast off the blankets. "I've lived with Indians, boy. Sure, some hate us. But a lot more don't. A lot of tribes would rather live in peace than lift our hair."

"Grandpa used to say we can't trust anyone with red skin, even the friendly ones. He said they're all heathens."

"Do you even know what that word means?"

"I told you I'm not stupid. It means they don't believe in God. They don't go to church or read the Bible or anything."

"Some do. Some convert. But most have their own religion. It's not the same but it's religion."

"Our religion is better, my ma says. If redskins lived like we do, there wouldn't be any blood spilled."

Fargo sighed. Arguing was pointless. The boy had had hate pounded into his head from an early age, and nothing Fargo could say or do would change his outlook.

Suddenly the wagon gave a lurch. Fargo steadied himself and moved to the front. "Did you hit a log?" he joked.

Rachel squealed, "You're awake!" and grasped his hand. "I was beginning to think you would sleep the whole day away."

Fargo wouldn't mind more rest but he elected to stay up. "Have I missed anything?"

"A lot of bumps," Lester said. "Martha thought she saw some smoke to the east a while ago. I looked but didn't see any."

"I saw it as clear as anything," Martha insisted. "I can't help it if my eyes are better than his."

"Was it campfire smoke or smoke signals?" Fargo asked.

"I'm afraid I wouldn't know the difference," Martha answered.

"Campfire smoke rises straight up. Smoke signals rise in puffs or small clouds," Fargo explained.

"Oh. In that case it was campfire smoke. More gold hunters, I'd wager."

Fargo hoped not. The Nez Perce were riled enough as it was. "Any chance you've changed your mind about the Payette River Valley?" he said to Lester.

The big farmer chuckled. "You never give up, do you? Why can't you understand what this means to us?"

"Why can't you understand that all of you could be massacred?" Fargo rejoined.

Lester half turned in the seat. "The Nez Perce wouldn't dare try. We have too many men and too many guns."

"You could have an entire regiment of troops and it wouldn't be enough," Fargo said.

"There you go again."

"I'm just trying to save your hides."

"And I appreciate that. But I think that once I've sat down with their chiefs for a parley, they will come to terms. We're prepared to offer the Nez Perce a third of the crops we harvest. That's fair, isn't it?"

"They might want something else."

"Like what?"

"The land you're taking from them."

"They have so much, I doubt they will begrudge us one valley," Lester predicted.

Fargo frowned. Once again arguing was pointless. Lester Winston had never been west of the Mississippi River, yet he thought he knew the Nez Perce better than someone who had lived on the frontier for years.

"Don't look so glum. Be happy for us. We're happy. Our dream is about to come true."

"You're a fool."

Lester lost some of his good mood. "I'll forgive you the slur. But don't make a habit of it. I have the best interests of my people at heart, and we will not be denied."

"Even if it gets you all killed?"

"Enough. We have listened to you and you have our answer. Be considerate enough to drop the subject."

Fargo got in one last lick. "I'll be considerate enough to bury you, too."

11

Days of slow travel. Nights of hot passion.

That was how Skye Fargo spent the next three days. The farmers treated him as a friend. If anyone regarded his nightly "walks" with Rachel as improper, they were polite enough not to say anything. It didn't occur to Fargo why until the third evening. He had just eaten his supper and was downing his third cup of coffee when Billy grinned at him and made a remark that explained everything.

"My sis sure will be busy at the stove, the way you stuff food down."

"The stove?" Fargo repeated.

Billy nodded. "When you're hitched. I heard Ma say as how she hopes you'll ask Rachel soon."

Fargo nearly choked on the coffee.

"Pa says you'll make a fine son-in-law. He likes that you're not green behind the ears. His own words." Billy grinned. "Ma says she figures she'll be a grandma before she can blink."

"Hell."

Billy's eyes narrowed. "Why do you have that funny look? Are you sick or something?"

"My coffee went down the wrong pipe."

"I've done that before. With milk. Once it came back out my nose. Don't you hate it when that happens?"

Fargo should have seen it sooner. The settlers were being so nice because they expected him to do the right thing. They expected him to wed Rachel. He wondered what Rachel thought. He'd made it plain to her that he

79

wasn't ready to be tied down. She'd said she understood. But women could say one thing and feel another. Could well be, she secretly hoped he would change his mind and pop the question. "Damn."

"What was that?" Billy asked.

"Yes, I hate it when that happens."

Victor Gore was friendly to him, too. Gore acted genuinely grateful to Fargo for helping with the Nez Perce. He came over as Billy was skipping off.

"Tomorrow is the big day. We'll reach the valley at last. I can't wait, Mr. Fargo. I will finally be able to get on about my own business."

"What would that be?"

"Why, I've already told you. Visiting my old trapping haunts."

"You're not sticking around to help the farmers settle in?"

"I doubt they need my aid. Winston and his people are capable folk. That is the way with farmers. They rely on the strength in their arms and the guidance of the Lord. But not me. I learned long ago that life is a roll of the dice. I'm rolling the die now by coming back here."

"How do you mean?"

"Oh, only that all of us have taken our lives in our hands, what with the Nez Perce and all."

"What about Rinson and his bunch? Will they go off with you or stay with the settlers?"

"Why would they stay? They were hired to see Lester's bunch safely to the valley. That's all. Once they've been paid the rest of their fee, I imagine they'll be on their way."

Fargo scowled. It would leave the settlers at the mercy of the Nez Perce, who were not in a merciful mood of late.

"You seem mad. But I assure you it was all worked out before we left Fort Bridger. Rinson made the conditions clear to Winston and his people. I was there. I heard every word."

"You know what will happen, don't you, when the Nez Perce find whites have moved in?"

Victor grimly nodded. "I warned Lester. You warned Lester. But he refuses to listen. I was puzzled at first. I thought he must be the most stubborn man on the planet."

It had been Fargo's experience that stubborn and stupid often went hand in hand.

"Whether it's that, or his faith that the Almighty will protect them, or some other reason, I've never met anyone so insistent on not taking advice when it's offered."

"Thinking like that can get them wiped out."

"You know that and I know that. But what can we say to someone who goes through life with blinders on?" Victor shook his head. "Some people believe only what they want to believe. You can talk to them until you are blue in the face and everything you say will go in one ear and bounce out again."

Fargo sighed.

"I never meant for the farmers to come here. A simple remark on my part about how fine the valley was, and Lester seized on it like a dog on a bone. He regards it as some sort of new Eden."

Fargo gazed across the circle at where the fiddler was warming up for the nightly festivities. "Some people never learn."

"No, they don't," Gore agreed. "And there is nothing the rest of us can do. My own conscience is clear."

As for Rinson and company, they pretty much left Fargo alone those three days. No more spying on him during the day and keeping watch on him at night. They seemed to have accepted the fact that the settlers didn't mind having him along. Even Slag and Perkins ignored him.

There was no trace of the Nez Perce, and for that Fargo was thankful.

At last the big morning arrived.

The covered wagons were winding along the Payette River. The farmers were excited that their long trek was almost at an end. Victor Gore was excited that soon he would be back in his old haunts. Even the so-called protectors showed signs of being excited, although what they had to be excited about, Fargo couldn't guess. Unless it was that soon they would get the rest of the money they were due and could return to Fort Bridger.

Fargo was riding alongside the Winston's wagon when Victor Gore came galloping back to excitedly report that he had spotted the mouth of the valley ahead. Word spread. The farmers lashed their teams to go faster, and before long a broad valley spread out before their eager eyes. Oval shaped, it was everything Gore said it would be: lush with grass, with timbered slopes on three sides, plenty of wood for cabins and barns, and plenty of game for the pot. Fargo had to admit it was ideal.

The farmers brought their wagons to a stop in the middle of the valley and hopped down to gaze in heart-felt joy at their new home. Lester Winston scooped up a handful of dirt. He smelled it, and ran it through his fingers, and announced that it was some of the richest soil he'd ever seen.

Fargo didn't share in the general elation. The valley was too open. Should the Nez Perce attack in force, the farmers wouldn't stand a prayer. The wooded slopes would provide ideal cover for a war party to sneak in close and spy on the whites, waiting for the right moment to attack. But he didn't voice his worries to Lester Winston. He would be wasting his breath.

Rachel came over and gleefully clasped his hands. "Isn't it glorious?" she asked, her eyes alight with delight.

"If you've seen one valley, you've pretty much seen them all."

"You don't understand. This is the start of a dream for us. We have a lot at stake here, more than you can imagine. If all goes as my pa has planned, before too long we'll have everything we've ever wanted. A new home. A new farm. We'll be much better off than we were in Ohio."

"You could also be dead."

Rachel drew back, her eyebrow arching. "What has gotten into you? Why can't you share in our joy?"

Fargo motioned at the green grass that covered the valley floor. "You see ten cabins and barns. I see bleached bones picked clean by the buzzards."

"My goodness. Can you be any more gloomy? But I refuse to let you spoil this moment for me." Rachel smiled and raised an arm to the azure sky. "I'm so happy, I want to shout."

"Rachel . . ." Fargo began, but she thrust a hand at him.

"Don't. It's about the Nez Perce, isn't it? I'm touched that you're so worried, but you carry it too far."

Fargo had said his last word on the subject. He'd tried with her father and mother and he had tried with her, and all they did was smile and seek refuge in denial. Whatever happened now was on their heads.

Rinson, Slag and Perkins were huddled with the rest of the protectors. From their angry gestures and low but sharp voices, they were in heated argument. Fargo tried to catch what they were saying. He started to drift toward them when suddenly Rinson, Slag and Perkins broke from the rest and came toward the farmers.

Rinson held out his palm to Lester Winston. "It's time. We got you here safe, like we promised. Now pay us what is due."

"You have done fine, sir," Winston told him. "We have no complaints. Give me a minute to fetch my poke from my wagon."

Several farmers added their compliments.

"When will you be leaving us?" the farmer named Harvey asked.

"We haven't decided yet," Rinson answered.

"You're welcome to stay as long as you want," another said.

"We're planning to celebrate," a third farmer revealed. "Tonight or tomorrow night. The ladies will bake cakes and cookies. And Sam will play his fiddle. We'll have us a grand time."

"Are you inviting the Nez Perce?" Fargo asked.

"Why on earth would we do that?"

Just then Lester Winston returned. "That's not a bad idea, Mr. Fargo. It would show them we have peaceable intentions." He opened his poke and commenced to count out coins.

Fargo scanned the surrounding mountains. It was only a matter of time before the Nez Perce showed up. "You'll be lucky if they don't slit your throats on sight."

"None of that kind of talk in front of the ladies and the children, if you please," Lester chided him. "You'll scare them."

"It would help if *someone* was scared," Fargo said.

As soon as Rinson had the money, he divided it among the other protectors. Fargo seemed to be the only one who noticed that they weren't nearly as happy about being paid as they should be. It was peculiar.

Lester jingled the few coins left in his poke. "There's not much left but we'll fill our pokes again real soon." He gave a slight start. "That is, after we've grown our crops and taken them to market."

"Where?" Fargo asked.

"Why, to Fort Bridger, of course. Or maybe to Fort Laramie. From there we can send our surplus east on freight wagons."

"You have it all thought out."

"I like to think so, yes."

Fargo was being sarcastic but Winston didn't notice. "That's a long way to ship corn or wheat. And vegetables would rot."

"We're well aware of that," Winston said. "Which is why we have intended from the start that when we got to Oregon we would try a whole new crop. One that won't spoil on its way to market." He looked about them. "I suppose they would grow just as well here as in Oregon."

"What is this wonder called?"

Lester smiled and swelled out his chest in pride at their brainstorm. "Potatoes."

"What?"

"You heard me. We're going to grow potatoes."

Fargo stared.

"I'm serious. Potatoes don't need a long growing season and they keep for a long time. They're perfect."

"You're loco. Why would people back East buy potatoes from way out here when they can grow their own?"

Lester had more to say, but just then Rinson came back. Slag and Perkins were at his elbows.

"What is it?" Lester asked. "Was my count off?"

"No, your count was fine," the hawk-faced man said. "But we've been talking it over and we've decided we'll stick around for a spell."

"You will?"

Fargo was as surprised as Winston.

"Our horses can use the rest. So can we. And if the Nez Perce show up, they'll be less likely to attack."

"I can't tell you how grateful we are," Lester said. In his enthusiasm he clapped Rinson on the arm. "With you watching over our families, we'll be free to get that much more work done."

"I'm glad you like the idea."

Fargo said nothing. But Rinson and his friends didn't strike him as charitable sorts.

"Let me go spread the news." Lester hustled away with Harvey and the others.

Rinson shifted toward Fargo. "What about you, mister? I take it you'll be on your way soon?"

"When I'm good and ready."

"Damn, you're prickly. But if I was in your boots, I'd stick around, too, what with that gal being so sweet on you."

"Be careful," Fargo said.

Rinson didn't take offense. "All I'm saying is that she's as fine a filly as I've ever set eyes on."

Perkins said, "Better ask her to be yours before one of the sons of one of these dirt-pushers gets the notion."

Slag bobbed his chin. "Stay as long as you want, mister. It's fine by us. We don't hold grudges."

The three grinned and walked off.

Fargo was inclined to pinch himself to be sure he was awake. What in hell was that all about? he wondered. He didn't buy for a minute that those three had sheathed their claws. They were up to something. But what?

Then Victor Gore came around a wagon. "Fargo! There you are. Lester just told me that Rinson and his men have decided to stay around awhile."

"That's the rumor."

"Marvelous. Just marvelous. I'm free to roam about, then, and not have to worry about them." Victor gleefully rubbed his palms together. "Yes, sir. Things have worked out better than I dared hope."

12

The first attempt on Fargo's life took place several days later, late in the afternoon.

During that time the farmers held a lot of meetings. Lester told Fargo they were deciding how to divide up the valley. "We figure we'll give each lot a number and then draw the number out of a hat."

For some reason Winston laughed after he said that.

As for Rinson and the "protectors," they kept busy patrolling the valley's perimeter for sign of hostiles during the day, and at night they took turns standing guard.

Little was seen of Victor Gore. Each morning he rode out at first light and didn't return until near sundown. When Billy asked what he was doing, Gore explained that he was visiting places he had trapped years ago. Billy mentioned that he was amazed Gore could find them again after so many years, and Gore said there was one spot in particular he was anxious to revisit, but so far he hadn't been able to locate it.

"But I will. Mark my words. It's the most important of all."

Fargo didn't bother to ask what was so special about a spot where Gore had pulled dead beaver out of the water.

Those first days Gore came back tired and glum. He didn't talk much at supper, except to say that a lot had changed, and many of the landmarks he remembered were hard to locate.

The second evening Gore was in even worse spirits. He told the Winstons he had traveled through some dreadfully thick country and was worn out. "The only good note is that the beaver are thriving again. I thought we had trapped them out, but by God, there are as many now as there were back then."

At one time, it had been widely feared that beaver had been trapped to the edge of extinction. But once the fur trade dwindled and prime skins were no longer in demand, the beaver population quickly recovered.

"I'm so happy I could bust," Vincent Gore declared.

Fargo mostly hunted. There were a lot of mouths to feed, a lot of supper pots to fill with fresh meat. From morning until twilight he roved the surrounding mountains. He shot two deer the first day, three the second. The third day, toward the middle of the afternoon, he came on tracks made by a big buck. Fresh tracks, with the scent of the buck's urine strong in the air.

Shucking the Henry from the saddle scabbard, Fargo stalked it, riding slowly and quietly.

He was over a mile from the valley. Now and then he caught sight of it far below.

The sun was warm on his face. Other than a few vagrant gusts, the wind was still. He had not come across any sign of the Nez Perce.

All was peaceful.

Fargo started up another slope. He saw where the buck had abruptly veered off and wondered why. A possible explanation came the next moment when a leaden hornet buzzed his ear at the same split instant that a rifle cracked below him.

The only reason the would-be killer missed was because Fargo had started to turn his head in the direction the buck had gone.

Instinctively, Fargo bent low and used his spurs. Within seconds he was in among white pines. Drawing rein, he dismounted and crept to where he could see the part of the slope where the shot came from. He patiently probed every shadowed patch and thicket but saw no one.

Suspecting the bushwhacker was gone, Fargo climbed

on the Ovaro and circled lower until he came to his own back trail. As he expected, he found the tracks of another horse. A shod horse.

The bushwhacker was a white man. Indians didn't ride shod horses. And since there were no other whites within five hundred miles, it had to be someone from the valley. Since he couldn't see any of the farmers trying to kill him, that cut the likely suspects to eight: one of Rinson's protectors. But which one? And why, for God's sake?

The attempt was doubly puzzling because Rinson and company had left him alone for so long. They seemed to have accepted the fact he was going to stick around.

Fargo backtracked the killer. The man had shadowed him a long way, staying well back so Fargo wouldn't spot him.

Fargo checked behind him often. Now and again he hid and waited to see if he was being followed.

Along about sundown Fargo came to the valley floor. As was his habit, he stripped the Ovaro and spread out his blankets near the Winstons' wagon. For the time being, for their mutual protection, the farmers were keeping their wagons circled in the middle of the valley. Until they got their cabins built, they were easy targets.

Fargo helped himself to coffee and sat with his back to his saddle, peering out from under his hat brim. One of Rinson's men was standing guard over the horse herd, another was walking the circle. The rest were huddled around a fire, talking and joking. None of them so much as glanced in his direction.

Discovering which one had tried to kill him would take some doing.

The sun was practically gone when Victor Gore showed up. He was whistling as he rode in, and he greeted the farmers jovially.

Then it happened.

The only reason Fargo noticed was because he was watching the protectors. He saw Rinson and Slag and Perkins glance up. He saw Rinson give Vincent Gore a pointed look. He saw Gore nod, a barely perceptible bob of the chin that no one else caught. And he saw Rinson turn to Slag and Perkins and say something that brought huge grins to their faces.

What the hell was that all about? Fargo wondered. He went on sipping coffee, and when Gore came over, greeted him with, "You're in a good mood."

"Why wouldn't I be?" Gore rejoined. "I love this part of the country. It is everything I remember it being."

"Do you remember the part where Indians kill white men who invade their land?"

"Honestly, Mr. Fargo. Give it a rest. We haven't seen hide nor hair of the Nez Perce, and frankly, I'm beginning to think we never will. In all the thousands of square miles of territory they roam, we are a needle in a haystack."

Fargo swallowed more coffee, then casually asked, "How long before you head back to civilization?"

Gore blinked. "I haven't given it much thought. It could be a couple of weeks. Maybe longer." He paused. "How about you? When do you plan to get on with your own life?"

"When I'm sure these people are safe."

"But according to you, they never will be. They are a massacre waiting to happen."

"You took the words right out of my mouth."

Victor grinned. "You should have been born a chicken. You make a great mother hen."

No sooner did the old trapper wander off than Rachel sank down and brazenly put her hand on Fargo's knee. "How was your day?"

"You're beginning to sound like a wife."

Rachel removed her hand and said uncertainly, "What's the matter? You sound mad."

"Not at you," Fargo assured her. After making sure no one could overhear, he told her about the attempt to ambush him.

"Why would anyone do such a thing?" Rachel was

shocked. "I'll go tell my pa and he'll get to the bottom of it."

"No," Fargo said, snagging her wrist as she went to stand. "The only one who is to know is you, and then only so you can keep your eyes peeled when I'm off hunting."

Rachel leaned closer, her breath warm on his neck. "Peeled for what?"

"Them." Fargo nodded at Rinson and his men. "Their comings and goings. Keep track of who goes where and when, and let me know when I get back."

"That's easy enough."

"Don't let them catch on," Fargo warned.

"What will they do? Try to kill me? I very much doubt it. Besides, what purpose would it serve? If you ask me, whoever it was who took a shot at you was acting on their own behalf." Rachel gnawed her lower lip. "I bet it was Slag or Perkins. Neither of them likes you."

"Just be careful," Fargo stressed.

Grinning impishly, Rachel squeezed his leg. "Why, kind sir, does this mean you care?"

Before Fargo could answer, Martha Winston was in front of them, and she wasn't happy. "How many times must I tell you, daughter? Look at yourself. Sitting there with your hand on Mr. Fargo's leg, cozying up to him for everyone to see."

"Oh, Ma," Rachel began.

"Don't Ma me. Take your hand off his leg right this second. It's bad enough you're the talk of the camp. I won't have you acting the hussy where everyone can see."

"She hasn't done anything to be ashamed of," Fargo came to Rachel's defense.

"Spare me your lies, Mr. Fargo," Martha said sharply. "You seem to forget we are God-fearing folk. We live by the Bible. To some that might seem silly. But we try to do what's right, and it's not right for an unmarried woman to carry on with a man the way my daughter has been carrying on with you. I haven't said anything until now because I've hoped and prayed that you would propose. But that's not going to happen, is it?"

Fargo didn't answer.

"I didn't think so. But at least you're not a hypocrite. You haven't promised her the moon to get under her skirts. Why buy the cow when you can have the milk for free?"

"Ma!" Rachel exclaimed.

"Oh, please. I'm a married woman with two children. When I was your age I felt what you're feeling. But I never gave in, not until I said 'I do.' That's the difference between right and wrong. I won't cast stones, but I wish to heaven Mr. Fargo would leave so we can get on with our lives and find you a man to call your very own."

This was the first inkling Fargo had that Rachel's mother felt this way. "I can't leave just yet."

Martha misconstrued. "Of course not. You have a good thing going here. But I ask you to reconsider. For our sakes. The sooner we are shed of you, the better. The longer you drag this out, the more harm it will do to Rachel's reputation."

Rachel said, "I don't care about that."

"But I *do*. Someone has to watch out for you. Or hasn't it occurred to you that you are harming your prospects of getting a husband?"

"That's ridiculous."

"Is it? Most men don't want loose women for wives. You best hope your reputation doesn't spread or you're liable to end your days alone and miserable, the price of your folly."

Tears welled in Rachel's eyes. "How can you talk to me like this?"

"If I don't, who will? Certainly not your father. He pretends to turn a blind eye to your shenanigans but deep down he's hurt."

Rachel bowed her head.

"As for you," Martha said to Fargo. "Haven't you

done enough harm? Can't you control your urges and leave us be?"

"Hell," Fargo said.

"I will only say this once," Martha said. "And keep in mind I know how to use a gun. I've hunted game, and shot ducks on the wing."

Fargo had a disturbing thought.

Martha turned. "I've said my piece." Wheeling, she walked off, her back as rigid as a ramrod.

"She's right," Rachel said softly. "I didn't give it any thought. But God help me, she's right." She slowly stood. "Excuse me. I need to be alone for a while. I hope you don't mind."

"Go ahead," Fargo said.

Rachel walked away, her head bowed.

A few glances were thrown Fargo's way by those who overheard Martha's tirade. Rather than sit there and be stared at, Fargo got up and walked about to stretch his legs, and to think. It was preposterous, his suspicion, but stranger things had happened. He was so deep in thought that he nearly collided with someone who suddenly stepped in front of him.

"We need to talk," Rinson said.

"You, too?"

"What?" Rinson lowered his voice. "Did you see any Injun sign when you were out hunting today?"

"No."

"One of my men did. He claims he saw a red devil spying on the farmers from the woods at the end of the valley."

"Your man didn't shoot him?"

"We don't want trouble with the Nez Perce if we can avoid it. Not for our sakes. For the settlers. They're the ones who have to live here after we're gone. Unless we're attacked, we'll leave the Nez Perce be."

"That's damned decent of you," Fargo said.

"I don't much like your tone. But I wanted you to know, just in case my man wasn't seeing things."

"I'm obliged."

Rinson hooked his thumbs in his gun belt. "See? We can get along if we try."

Fargo watched the hawk-faced hardcase saunter back to his friends. First Gore, then Martha, now this. Add the Nez Perce into the mix, and he better have eyes in the back of his head or there was a good likelihood he would end up with a bullet in the brain or an arrow between his shoulder blades.

13

The second attempt to kill him came the next morning.

Fargo was up at daybreak, as usual, and ate breakfast with the Winstons, as usual. Martha was cold to him. Rachel was withdrawn. Lester talked about downing timber for their cabins, and how he couldn't wait to break soil and plant crops. Billy chattered about an eagle he had seen and possible wolf tracks the boys found.

Fargo was tightening the Ovaro's cinch when the scent of lilacs wreathed him.

Rachel had a shawl over her shoulders and a bonnet on her head. "I've been thinking over what my mother said to us."

"And?" Fargo prompted when she didn't go on.

"I'm sorry she's so upset. But I'm past the age where she can tell me what to do. I can do as I please and it pleases me to be with you."

Fargo gave the cinch a final tug.

"As for people talking behind my back, that can't be helped. If they want to think I'm a hussy, so be it. I know I'm not."

"You'll have to live with them after I'm gone."

"So? Either they accept me as I am or they can go to Hades and I'll go live in a city somewhere. I hear a woman can make it on her own if she's willing to work hard."

Fargo reached for the saddle horn but Rachel put a hand on his arm.

"I just don't want you thinking it's over between us because of Ma. It's not, is it?"

"I'm not ready to leave just yet."

"Good. Because I was hoping we can go for another stroll tonight after supper. Just the two of us." Rachel smiled shyly. "I can't help it if I can't get enough of you."

Amused, Fargo said, "A walk will be fine." He had met women like her before. Once their passion was kindled, it became a roaring fire.

"One other thing," Rachel said, and kissed him on the cheek. "Be careful today, will you?"

"Always." Fargo caught Martha glaring at him. Smiling at her, her stepped into the stirrups.

A few farmers waved as he rode out. They appreciated the hunting he did since they didn't have time to do it themselves. Suddenly Fargo came on Perkins, who was riding the perimeter. To his mild surprise, Perkins smiled.

"Morning."

Fargo grunted.

"Good luck on your hunt. Maybe you can get an elk. One of these plow-pushers was saying as how he saw some at the far end of the valley yesterday."

"I can't make any promises." Fargo had heard the same thing from Lester, and did, in fact, intend to go see if he could find them. "If you see Gore, tell him I might not be back until late."

"He rode out a while ago."

"Awful early," Fargo remarked.

"You know how he is. I guess there's a lot of country he's hankering to see again."

"Must be." Fargo clucked to the Ovaro and didn't look back. He scanned the valley for sign of Gore but the old man was long gone.

The elk had left plenty of tracks. They couldn't help it, as huge and heavy as they were. Fargo followed them up a long slope to a low ridge half a mile up. He was intent on reading the sign as he neared a large boulder. By sheer chance he happened to glance right at the boulder as a man came vaulting up and over with a blade glinting in his hand.

It was one of Rinson's men—short, stocky, with a pockmarked face and missing front teeth.

Fargo went for his Colt but he was a shade too late. The man slammed into him, smashing him from the saddle, while simultaneously stabbing at his throat. Fargo jerked aside and the knife missed. They tumbled and the man tried again to bury his blade. They hit hard and Fargo pushed away and up into a crouch, palming his Arkansas toothpick.

"Damn you," the man snarled, and came at him again.

Fargo didn't know his name. He'd barely spoken two words to him the whole time he had been with the wagon train. Yet here the man was, fiercely determined to kill him.

The blade flashed at Fargo's throat. He dived, rolled toward the man instead of away from him, and streaked the toothpick up and out.

A bleat of surprise greeted the thrust. That, and a sudden line of red on the man's shirt.

Fargo had missed his vitals. The man swore and slashed in a berserk fury, seeking to break through Fargo's guard and end their fight quickly. But Fargo was no slouch with a knife, himself. They stabbed, parried, cut, feinted. Steel rang on steel. Fargo's shoulder spiked with pain and he opened a wound on the other's thigh.

Breathing heavily, they circled. The man was wary now.

Fargo did something he normally wouldn't do. He spoke. "What is this about?"

"Go to hell."

"Is this Rinson's idea? Why does he want me dead?"

"If you only knew the truth," the man said.

"Suppose you enlighten me."

"Eat steel."

Again the man's blade flashed. This time he went for the heart. Fargo sidestepped, countered, felt the toothpick bite into flesh and was rewarded with more swearing.

"I won't kill you if you tell me why you're doing this."

Instead of answering, the man growled like a wild beast, and like a wild beast he threw himself forward with his knife weaving a tapestry of cold death.

Fargo was hard-pressed to avoid harm. He ducked a stab intended for his eye and speared the toothpick into the man's armpit. A yelp preceded a spurt of blood, and the man quickly skipped back out of reach.

Balanced on the balls of his feet, Fargo waited, the toothpick low down, dripping scarlet drops. "You'll bleed out fast if something isn't done."

"God damn you." The man glanced at the spreading stain on his shirt. "He said it would be easy."

"Who?"

"I can't say."

"Drop the knife and tell me and I'll do what I can to save you," Fargo offered.

The man hesitated.

"Was it you who shot at me yesterday?" Fargo asked to keep him talking.

"No. That was—"

A shot shattered the morning air.

The slug struck the man's brow with a loud *thwack*, snapping his head back and spinning him half around. Eyes wide, he tried to speak but all that came out of his throat was a whine and a gurgle. Then his knees buckled.

Fargo threw himself flat. He twisted but didn't see the shooter or even a puff of gun smoke. Scrambling under cover, he let the minutes drag by. Eventually, convinced the shooter was gone, he cautiously stood and moved to the dead man. He went through his pockets but all he found were a few coins and a folding knife.

Fargo had half a mind to storm back to the camp and pistol-whip Rinson. But the rest of the protectors wouldn't stand idly by. And there were too many of them for him to take on alone, not without an edge of some kind.

Fargo came up with a better idea.

Ordinarily, he would bury a body deep enough that the scavengers couldn't get at it. But since this son of a bitch had tried to kill him, he scooped out a shallow grave using a broken tree limb. Unbuckling the man's gun belt, he rolled the body into the hole and covered it with a thin layer of dirt. Coyotes and whatnot were bound to get at it, but they had to eat, too.

Five minutes was all it took to find the would-be killer's horse, a roan that didn't seem to care that a strange man had hold of the reins.

Fargo shoved the gun belt into the man's saddlebags. He led the roan to the Ovaro, climbed on, and continued tracking the elk. The extra horse would come in handy later.

By now it was obvious Rinson and company wanted him dead. The question remained: *Why?* What were they up to, Fargo wondered, that they wanted him out of the way? He never believed for a minute that they were sticking around out of the goodness of their hearts. That business about staying to protect the farmers was so much hogwash.

Another question: What part did Vincent Gore play in all of this? Was the old trapper up to something? Or was he just as he seemed?

In disgust, Fargo gave a toss of his head. He needed answers. But getting them might take some doing.

Elk, like deer, were most active at dawn and dusk and liked to lie up during the day. Fargo figured the herd he was after had sought out cover higher up, and he was right. An hour's climb brought him to a grassy meadow where there was twice as much elk sign as lower down. A meadow bordered by the heavy growth they favored.

Tying both horses to a tree, Fargo slid the Henry from the scabbard and stalked his quarry on foot. He made less noise that way, and he needed to catch the elk unaware. For all their size and bulk, they were remarkably quick-hoofed, and could melt into the vegetation in the bat of an eye.

As it was, Fargo almost stalked right by them. They knew he was there, and they were as still as statues until he was practically on top of them. Then the twitch of an ear gave a cow away, and when Fargo whirled and brought up the Henry, the entire herd was up and in motion.

The males were five feet high at the shoulder and close to ten feet long, and could weigh over a thousand pounds. Females were smaller but still weighed between six and seven hundred pounds. A lot of meat was packed on their big bones, meat the settlers could use in the coming months if it was properly cured and salted.

Since it was summer, antlers had sprouted on the males, and it was easy for Fargo to pick a young one. At the shot, the young bull went down. But it was immediately back up and running as if the slug had just grazed it.

Fargo fixed a bead on its head. Working the lever as fast as he could, he banged off three swift shots and at the third the elk went down and this time it stayed down.

The rest went crashing off through the brush.

In no hurry, Fargo spent all afternoon skinning and carving and tying the meat on the roan. He packed on as much as he could but there was still plenty left. He wrapped as much as he could in what was left of the hide and covered it, intending to come back the next day.

Butchering was blood-drenched, gory work. Fargo was an old hand at it but he still got blood all over him and on his buckskins.

Once again the sun was balanced on the rim of the world when Fargo bent the Ovaro's steps toward the valley far below. It was an uncomfortable feeling, riding back into a nest of vipers. He reminded himself that the farmers weren't the snakes in the grass. They were innocents, caught up in God-knew-what. He would do what he could for them but it might not be enough.

Fargo never ceased to be amazed at how pigheaded people could be. He'd tried to talk them out of coming. Gore had tried to talk them out of coming. But would they listen? No. They had their minds made up and nothing anyone could say or do would change things.

Shadows dappled the pine-needle-strewn ground. A jay squawked and flew off. Later on a pair of ravens flew overhead, the beat of their wings clear and distinct.

Fargo breathed deep of the dank scent of the forest, and was for the moment content. Were it not for his fondness for whiskey, cards and women, he wouldn't mind spending the rest of his days in the wild. He would as soon sleep under the stars as in a bed and eat roast venison over a roaring fire as eat a slab of beef at a restaurant.

Campfires glowed in the circle. Sentries had been posted. The women tended supper pots while the children played and the men rested from their labors, puffing on pipes or thick cigars.

Fargo's arrival created a stir. Lester Winston took charge of the elk meat, saying, "We're obliged. We won't go hungry for a coon's age, thanks to you."

Fargo turned and found his way blocked by the usual three: Rinson, Slag and Perkins. Two other protectors were with them but standing well back, hands near their revolvers. "You're in my way."

"We need to talk," Rinson said.

"Not now. I'm tired."

"One of my men has gone missing. Clark is his name. And I figure you know what happened to him."

"You figure wrong."

"Oh?" Rinson nodded at where the farmers were untying the elk meat from the roan. "That's Clark's horse."

"I wondered whose it was. I found it all by itself up in the mountains and brought it back with me."

"You didn't see hide nor hair of Clark?" Slag asked.

"Can't say as I did, no." Fargo gestured. "Now are you going to move or do I have to move you?"

Perkins chuckled. "I'd like to see you try."

"Enough," Rinson snapped. "No more of that. Not now. Not here. Understood?"

"I savvy," Perkins said resentfully.

"You're lucky, mister," Skag said to Fargo.

Fargo was about to walk on when the sentry gave a shout and hooves drummed. Into the circle galloped Vincent Gore. In his excitement, Gore nearly rode a woman down. But it was what he shouted that galvanized everyone into rushing to their wagons and arming themselves.

"The Nez Perce are coming!"

14

Rifles bristled from wagon seats, from under the wagons, from behind the wagons. For over an hour the settlers were tense with dread, awaiting an attack. But the Nez Perce didn't show. The sky darkened and night fell, and nothing happened.

"I don't understand it," Victor Gore said. "They chased me for miles. They were only a few hundred yards behind me when I reached this valley."

"Maybe they know we're here," Lester Winston speculated. "Maybe they are off in the woods right this minute, watching us."

Fargo was skeptical. The Nez Perce had no reason to fear the farmers, not if there were as many warriors as Gore claimed. "How many were there again?" he asked to be certain.

"I couldn't count them, what with riding for my life, but I'd be willing to swear on a stack of Bibles there were seventy or more."

"That's a sizable war party," Rinson remarked.

Too sizable, in Fargo's estimation. The only reason a war party would be that large was if the Nez Perce were on a raid against an enemy village.

"Strange they haven't shown," a farmer mentioned from his roost on a wagon.

"They better come soon," a woman said. "My nerves are frayed. I can't take this waiting."

"Someone should go see where they got to," Rinson proposed.

"I agree," Gore said. "And since I was the fool who

led them here, I'll go." The old trapper turned toward his horse.

As they had done before, all eyes fixed on Fargo. Inwardly he swore but out loud he said, "It should be me who goes. I stand a better chance of making it back with my hair."

Gore grinned. "This is no time for false bravery. I'll gladly let you do it in my stead."

Fargo made for the Ovaro. "Me and my big mouth," he muttered, then realized he wasn't alone.

"Be careful, Skye," Rachel urged. "There's no telling what they will do if they get their hands on you."

Fargo hoped that Winter Wolf, the old warrior he had met, was with them. Winter Wolf might palaver rather than have him killed. Not that it would do much good. The Nez Perce weren't about to let the farmers stay. "You were idiots to come here."

"Here we go again!"

"If it were up to me, I'd run the whole bunch of you clear back to the Mississippi River."

"How can you talk like that after we've let you stay with us and my ma has cooked your meals and all?"

Fargo hurriedly saddled. He was about done when Victor, Lester and Rinson drifted over.

"I'm sorry to have brought this on you," Gore said. "I was scared. I didn't think to try and lead them away."

Lester said, "Don't be so hard on yourself. Anyone would have done the same."

Not Fargo, but he didn't say so.

"If you want," Rinson spoke up, "I'll send a couple of my men with you. Slag and Perkins wouldn't mind going."

That was all Fargo needed, a war party in front of him and two killers at his back. "I'll go alone."

Anxious faces were pale blots in the dark as Fargo brought the Ovaro to a gap between wagons and forked leather. The saddle creaked under him, and then his boots were in the stirrups. "If I'm not back by sunup—" He didn't finish. He didn't need to.

"It won't come to that," Lester said. "Not if you don't let them get their hands on you."

Was it Fargo's imagination, or were there tears in Rachel's eyes? He touched his hat brim and rode out. The Indians were at the mouth of the valley, Gore claimed. But Fargo didn't head there. He reined wide to the right so he could come up on them through the forest. His skin prickling, he held the Ovaro to a walk. Less noise that way, and less chance of blundering into waiting warriors.

Fargo supposed he should be thankful he wasn't going up against Apaches. Compared to them, the Nez Perce were kittens. Riled kittens, with bows and lances instead of teeth and claws.

It took half an hour. Once there, Fargo looked and listened but the woodland lay peaceful under a crescent moon and the multitude of stars. Where the hell were they? he wondered.

The mouth of the valley was too broad, too open. Fargo skirted it, hugging the tree line.

Still no sign of the war party.

Fargo reasoned that they had gone into the forest on the other side. For him to cross the river and go after them was foolhardy, yet that's what he did. He hated being in the open. But he reached the woods without incident, and for long minutes prowled the benighted vegetation. The only living things he encountered were an owl that hooted at him from a high branch and a pair of spooked does that bounded off in fright.

No Nez Perce anywhere.

Drawing rein, Fargo stared off toward the distant ring of wagons. The farmers had kept the fires going and he could see several figures moving about. When it came to preserving their skin, they had all the sense of rocks. But there was no denying their gratefulness when he rode back and announced that he had searched long and hard and not found anything. "If the Nez Perce were there, they're gone."

"If?" Victor Gore said. "Surely you're not suggesting

I imagined them? I tell you, sir, it was a war party, and a big one, and I am lucky to be alive."

"No one doubts you," Lester said. "It's our guns. They're afraid to show themselves."

Fargo came close to laughing in his face. One thing the Nez Perce weren't, were cowards. Should they decide to wipe the settlers out, that's exactly what they would do. Guns or no guns.

"Well, I guess we should all get some sleep," Lester proposed. "We need our rest."

"My men will stand guard as always," Rinson said. "You have nothing to worry about with us watching over you."

Fargo knew better. But he turned in when the rest did and spent a fitful night tossing and turning. Toward morning he drifted off and dreamed about being caught by the Nez Perce and skinned alive. A gentle hand on his shoulder, shaking him, returned him to the world of the real.

"Good morning, handsome," Rachel said. "This is a switch. Usually you're up before any of us."

The sun was rising. Fargo cast off his blankets and sat up. Martha had a fire going and was preparing breakfast. Other women were doing the same. The men moved about, talking.

"You must have been tired."

"Not *that* tired," Fargo said in disgust. "I'll head out again as soon as I've had a bite to eat."

"No need," Rachel said. "Mr. Gore and Mr. Rinson have already gone off to find the war party. Mr. Rinson took most of his men with him."

"What?"

A single guard was walking the circle, a rifle in the crook of an elbow. As Fargo looked on, the man yawned and scratched himself.

"Mr. Gore said as how it wouldn't be fair to ask you to go out again." Rachel smiled sweetly. "Wasn't that nice of him?"

"What about Rinson and his curly wolves?"

"Why did you call them that? They've done so much on our behalf. We have no complaints."

"Did Gore ask them to go or did they offer?"

Rachel cocked her head and regarded him quizzically. "What difference does it make? But now that I think about it, Mr. Rinson allowed as how, if there was to be a fight with the Indians, he'd rather the blood was spilled somewhere else." She beamed. "I tell you, with protectors like them, we're in good hands."

"So far they haven't protected you from much." Fargo had done most of the work but they took the credit.

"The hostiles have left us be, haven't they? If you ask me, those curly wolves, as you call them, have proven themselves our friends. We should be thankful, not hold petty grudges."

Fargo saw nothing petty about having his throat slit but he held his tongue, and stood.

"Where are you off to?"

"They can't have much of a head start. I plan to catch up to them and talk sense into Gore."

"What on earth for? Need I remind you he has always been polite and courteous to you? That should count for something."

"That's the reason I'm going after him." Otherwise, Fargo would leave the stubborn cuss to whatever fate had in store. He set to work saddling the Ovaro and was about done when the unexpected reared again. He turned to pick up his saddlebags and discovered Lester and Martha Winston and two farmers armed with shotguns. "What's this?"

Martha said stiffly, "My daughter told us that you're going after Mr. Gore and the others."

"So?"

"We're sorry, but we can't let you do that," Lester said. "Victor has our best interests at heart."

"You don't understand."

Martha smiled a smile as cold as a mountain glacier. "Oh, but I flatter myself I do. You've made no secret of the fact you have lived with Indians from time to time. And you said yourself that the other night when you tangled with the Nez Perce, you went out of your way not to kill any of them."

"So?" Fargo didn't see where her questions were leading.

"So you're partial to those red devils. You care about them more than a white person should."

"You should hear yourself."

"And you should remember what color your skin is," Martha said with more than mild irritation. "We *want* Victor and Mr. Rinson to find that war party. We *want* Mr. Rinson to shoot as many as he must to convince the rest to stay away from our valley."

"You want a war, in other words." Fargo's disgust knew no bounds. "You pathetic wretches."

"There's no need for name-calling," Lester said.

Martha pointed a finger at him. "Don't make more of this than there is. The death of some Indians is a small price to pay for our future."

The woman really believed that. Fargo shook his head and said, "I'm going, and that's final."

"I was afraid you wouldn't agree." Martha motioned at Lester and Lester motioned at the two men and they raised their shotguns. "Would you be so kind as to hand over your six-shooter? And don't try to jump on your horse or you might be shot in the leg for your troubles."

"Don't do this," Fargo said.

"What choice do you leave us?" Martha asked. "Our welfare is at stake. We can't let you stand in our way."

Fargo fought down an urge to draw on them. They were farmers, not outlaws or gun sharks. He could probably drop both shotgun wielders. But all it would take was one blast from one of those twelve-gauge hand cannons and he would be blown to kingdom come. "After all I've done for you."

"Let's not be petty, shall we?"

Fargo tried one last appeal. "Does she do your talking for you now, Lester?"

The big farmer sheepishly looked away. "She's my wife, Mr. Fargo."

"That's no answer."

"Spoken like a man who has never been married. She's my woman and I do what I can to make her happy. If she doesn't want you to interfere with Mr. Gore and our protectors, then by the eternal, you won't."

"Hell, Lester. I gave you credit for more sense."

Martha said, "Your problem is that you keep forgetting white and red don't mix and never will."

Fargo's temper flared. She was a bigot on top of everything else. "Wish I'd known this sooner."

"You mustn't think ill of us," Martha tried to placate him. "Not until you've stood in our shoes. How can you expect us to stand idly by when your antics threaten to dash our hopes and prayers?"

That was when Fargo noticed the man Rinson had left behind standing only a dozen feet away, a smirk on his face. "Are you going to just stand there and do nothing?"

"It's between you and them, mister," the man replied. "I'm to keep an eye out for redskins. My boss didn't say anything about you."

Fargo had to submit to the indignity of having his Colt and Henry taken. He also had to stand there helpless as the Ovaro, still saddled, was led off to be put with the other horses.

"In case you have any notions about sneaking off," Martha said smugly.

The only notion Fargo had right that moment was to chuck her off a cliff, but there wasn't one handy. With those shotguns trained on him, he settled for stepping to the rear wheel and sinking down with his back to the spokes.

"That's not so bad, is it?" Martha said in a tone that suggested he was the same age as her Billy.

"Lady, you don't know what bad is," Fargo said, and let it go at that. Lester and Martha left, leaving one of the men with a shotgun to guard him. Fuming, he plucked at the grass. He didn't look up when familiar feet appeared.

"I'm sorry. I tried to get them not to do this to you. I practically begged. But they refused."

"Do you know what a thunderstorm is?" Fargo asked.

"Of course, silly. Why?"

"Because one is about to break, and when it does, all hell will break with it."

15

Fargo didn't eat much supper. He wasn't in the mood. He chewed a few pieces of venison and poked at the carrots, but that was it. He did drink coffee. A lot of coffee.

After they ate, the farmers gathered as they ordinarily did, and the man who played the fiddle soon had some dancing while the rest looked on and talked and laughed.

The farmer assigned as Fargo's guard looked on, too. His back to Fargo, he was particularly interested in one woman. His wife, as Fargo recalled, who danced a couple of times with another man. Each time, his guard looked fit to burst a vein.

By then it was dark enough.

Fargo palmed a fist-sized rock he had noticed earlier. He made sure no one was looking toward the Winston wagon, then slowly rose and struck his guard over the back of the head. Fargo didn't hit him hard enough to kill him, but he wasn't gentle about it, either.

Catching the man before he could fall, Fargo eased him to the ground and placed him against the rear wheel, making it appear the man was sleeping with his hands in his lap. Then, staying well out of the firelight, Fargo headed for the wagon where the farmers had put his Colt and Henry. Both were lying in plain sight.

Now that he was rearmed, Fargo half hoped someone would try to stop him. But no one did. The Ovaro, still saddled, was with the other horses. He shoved the Henry into the scabbard and swung up. At a walk he headed for the valley mouth, but he soon broke into a trot.

He looked back only once. The fiddle still twanged and gay figures swirled. He thought he saw Billy staring in his direction. Not that it mattered. They couldn't catch him.

Fargo rode to the Payette River. He let the Ovaro drink, then paralleled the river. When he had gone far enough, he entered the forest. He went only a short way and climbed down.

A cold camp had to suffice. He couldn't track at night. He would wait until first light and head out again.

Gore and Rinson hadn't returned to the valley. But the farmers weren't alarmed. Lester Winston told Fargo that Gore had mentioned they would be gone however long it took them to find the war party and drive the Nez Perce off. Lester, of course, believed him.

Not Fargo. He had been skeptical about Gore from the beginning. Yes, a lot of trappers were fond of the mountains, and yes, some of them dearly missed the old days. But no one would do as Gore had done and come from back East into country overrun by hostiles. Not unless there was more to it.

Some folks might say Fargo was too cynical. That he didn't trust people enough. But he'd learned the hard way that trusting too freely could get a man killed. It was akin to going up to a grizzly with open arms and a smile and expect the bear to be as friendly as a puppy.

Fargo suspected that Gore was up to something. Gore had another motive for coming back to the mountains. Exactly how the farmers fit in, Fargo wasn't sure yet. But it didn't bode well that Gore and Rinson left just one man to protect them and had gone off.

His saddle for a pillow, a canopy of glittering stars above, Fargo listened to the howls of wolves and once, close by, the cry of a fox. He soon dozed off and wasn't intruded on by man or beast. Up at the break of day, he went to the river and found what he was looking for—the tracks of Gore and the rest, heading deeper into the wilds.

But no tracks of any Nez Perce.

Gore wasn't chasing a war party. He was up to something else, and it was high time Fargo found out what.

In the distance reared a mountain, one among many, its peak a jagged outcropping that thrust at the sky like a spear about to draw blood. It was there the tracks led.

It was pushing noon when Fargo drew rein at the edge of some trees. Beyond was a narrow canyon that split the mountain like a wound. And from out of the canyon came the ping of metal on rock.

Fargo was about to venture into the open when movement warned him to stay put.

A man was keeping watch. He was behind a large boulder, but he came out and squinted up at the sun, acting bored.

Fargo slid down and tied the Ovaro. With the Henry in his left hand he sank onto his belly and snaked from cover to cover until he was near enough to the boulder to hear the man mutter.

Fargo crawled past the boulder to the slope to the top of the canyon. Suddenly hooves clattered. He quickly pressed flat.

"About time you got here," the man standing guard said.

"Don't start," the new arrival replied.

"You were supposed to relieve me an hour ago, Larson. Where the hell have you been?"

"He had me working the vein. I have blisters from using that damn pickax. But he won't let us stop. He says we have to get it all as quick as we can."

"He's Injun shy."

"I can't blame him there. Not if you've ever seen what these red devils do. I'm not hankering to have my eyes gouged out and my tongue cut off."

"They have no idea we're here. Everything is going just as we planned."

"As he planned, you mean," Larson said. "I've got to

hand it to him. Everything has worked out just as he said it would, except for that Fargo character sticking his nose in."

"Hell, we didn't need those plow-pushers. We went to a lot of trouble for nothing."

"Would you rather carry it all out on your back, Barnes? They have their use."

A saddle creaked as Larson dismounted, then creaked again as Barnes climbed on.

"Any sign of anything?"

"Not unless you count bugs and a hawk. I tell you, we're worried over nothing."

"Sure, Barnes. Sure."

Hooves clattered, and Larson was alone.

Fargo crawled higher. Brush and boulders allowed enough cover for him to soon be well above the canyon floor. Removing his hat, he risked a look.

Larson was leaning against the boulder and staring off down the mountain. In the other direction, the canyon bent at a sharp angle. From beyond that bend came the ping of pickaxes.

Fargo jammed his hat back on and resumed crawling. When he was high enough to see past the bend, he inched to the edge. And there they were. Gore, Rinson, Slag, Perkins and the other so-called protectors, working hard in the hot sun, chipping away at the real reason Gore came back to the Rockies after all these years.

From what Fargo could see of the vein, it was scores of yards long and inches wide. Gold, mixed with quartz, the yellow bright where the sun struck it. Enough ore to make a prospector's mouth water. Hundreds of thousands of dollars' worth for whoever got it out.

It confirmed Fargo's hunch. Victor Gore must have stumbled on the vein during his trapping days. But why it took Gore so long to come back was a puzzle. Fargo started to back away when a gun hammer clicked.

"Not so much as a twitch or you're a dead man."

Fargo recognized the voice. It was another "protector." He cursed himself for not counting those below.

"My handle is Stern. Do as I say and you'll live a while longer."

A gun muzzle gouged Fargo low in the back, hard.

"This here rifle of mine is a Sharps," Stern informed him. "Ever shot one, mister?"

"Plenty of times," Fargo said. He had owned a Sharps before he switched to the Henry.

"Then you know how big a hole it'll blow in you. I want you to do exactly as I say. Start by putting your arms out from your sides. All the way out, with your fingers flat on the ground where I can see them."

Fargo did as he was told. A slight tug at his hip told him Stern had relieved him of the Colt.

"I reckon you feel pretty stupid right about now."

"More than stupid," Fargo admitted.

"Our boss has been expecting you. That's why he sent me up here to keep a lookout."

The pressure on Fargo's spine eased. Stern had stepped back.

"Now, nice and slow, I want you to stand up. Leave your rifle where it is and keep your hands out from your sides."

Once again Fargo complied. It was just his luck that Stern was the kind who didn't take chances. "Suppose I need to scratch my nose?"

"Go right ahead. The last sound you hear will sound like thunder. And then you and your nose will be breathing dirt." He paused. "Now shut the hell up and take five steps. Keep your back to me. Try to turn and my trigger finger twitches."

Fargo heard a boot scrape. Out of the corner of his eye he saw Stern at the edge, looking down. Lean as a rail, with bushy eyebrows and a pointed chin, Stern cupped a hand to his mouth and bellowed Victor Gore's name.

The pickaxes stopped picking and all heads rose.

"Well, well, well," Gore shouted up, smiling broadly. "Bring him down! But be careful. I hear he's tricky."

"Tricky but dumb!" Stern hollered down.

Laughter floated up, causing Fargo's jaw muscles to twitch. He hated making a jackass of himself. It never once occurred to him that they'd expect him to do exactly as he had done. And it should have. He was getting too careless of late.

"Start walking," Stern instructed. "Keep those arms where they are or have a hole blown in you."

It was one of the longest walks of Fargo's life. Larson met them at the bottom. Together, he and Stern marched Fargo up the canyon and around the bend. The others were hard at work again, except for Victor Gore and Rinson. Both waited with smiles on their faces.

"Mr. Fargo!" Gore said good-naturedly. "I can't tell you how pleased I am to see you."

"Go to hell."

"I'm serious. I was worried you would prove to be a thorn in my side. But now that I have you in my power, as it were—" Gore chortled. "This has worked out better than I dared hope."

"Drop dead." Fargo was looking at Gore and didn't realize Rinson had whipped the Remington from its holster until the long barrel flashed at his temple. His head exploded in pain and pinpoints of light seemed to swirl in the air. Dimly, he was aware of his legs giving out and of falling to his hands and knees. Somehow he stayed conscious and looked up as Rinson raised the Remington to club him again.

"No!" Victor Gore barked, stepping between them.

"What the hell is the matter with you?" Rinson snapped. "You said yourself we won't be safe until this bastard is maggot bait."

"All in good time, my friend. I want a few words with him first. Go work the vein."

Rinson grit his teeth and hissed like a struck snake. "I should do to you like I just did to him."

"But you won't," Victor Gore confidently declared.

"We'll have the gold," Rinson said with a sweep of his other arm at the rock outcropping.

"Thanks to me," Gore said. "And if you go on doing as I say, you might just make it out of this alive."

Fargo's head was beginning to clear. It hurt like hell but the pinpoints of light had faded. He slowly sat and gingerly touched his temple. When he drew his fingers away, his fingertips were scarlet with wet blood.

Rinson walked off in a huff.

"Sorry about that." Victor Gore squatted, that friendly smile of his in place. But it was belied by the hard glitter in his eyes. "I didn't hear a thank-you, but you're welcome."

Fargo had to swallow twice to get his throat to work. "For what?"

"For the few extra minutes of life. You see, I really need to know if you were telling the truth about the O'Flynns. Or was it a lie and you were after me all along?"

Fargo wished his head would stop pounding. "You?"

"For leading that simpleton Winston and his people into Nez Perce country. The army has been trying to keep people out. And since you've scouted for them and done other work for the military, I hear, it hit me that maybe they sent you in." Gore's brow knit. "But then you made no attempt to stop us, which confused me considerably until it dawned on me that, incredible as it seemed, you'd figured out what I was up to."

Fargo stared at the others, feverishly working. "There had to be more to this than your old haunts."

"Ah. Then you did suspect?" Pleased with himself, Gore chuckled.

"How did you find it?" Fargo asked, nodding at the vein. He immediately regretted it; the throbbing grew worse.

"First things first." Gore straightened and beckoned to Perkins, who stopped chipping and hurried over. "Would you be so good as to tie Mr. Fargo's wrists and ankles?"

"I'll fetch my rope."

Fargo put his hands flat on the ground to push to his feet but Victor Gore produced a derringer. "Stay right where you are, if you please. We'll continue our talk in a minute. And when we're done, well." He wagged the derringer. "If it's any consolation, I'll make it quick. A bullet to the brain so there is little pain."

"You're all heart," Fargo said.

16

"Now where was I?" Victor Gore asked.

Fargo was on his side in the dirt. His hands were bound behind his back and his ankles had been tied. The rope was so tight on his wrists, his arms were starting to hurt. "You changed your mind. You were going to cut me loose and let me go."

Gore blinked, then threw back his head and roared. "That was a good one. Such spirit, when here you are about to meet your Maker."

The gold ore, Fargo noticed, was being put in burlap sacks. So far dozens of sacks had been heaped in piles, and the piles were steadily growing.

"No, Mr. Fargo. I'm afraid you stuck your nose in where you shouldn't have, and it will cost you dearly."

"There is one thing I'd like to know," Fargo said. "Why did it take you so long?"

"To come back, you mean? I'll get to that in a moment." Gore glanced at the workers, grunted in satisfaction, then said, "As you have guessed, I found the vein during my trapping days. Or, rather, a friend and I did. It was between trapping seasons, when we had free time to do as we pleased. I loved to explore, and he always tagged along. One day we weren't far from here, just riding along without a care, when we were set on by hostiles. Not the Nez Perce, by the way. Piegans. No doubt on a raid. And the moment they saw us, they whipped their horses and shrieked like banshees."

Fargo didn't doubt it. The Piegans were notorious for killing every white they came across.

"We fled, of course. And as fate would have it, our flight brought us to this very canyon. We thought we had given them the slip. But no sooner did we spot the vein than the red devils appeared on the rim above us, raining down arrows. We spurred our mounts to escape but one of the shafts struck my friend in the eye." Gore stopped, and shuddered. "I saw him get hit. I saw the tip pierce his socket and burst out the back of his head. And then I rode like a madman up the canyon and out the far end. I didn't stop until I'd left those red demons far behind."

"Too bad," Fargo said.

"What?" Gore looked at him, and laughed. "Oh. Too bad I got away? But I did, and I couldn't stop thinking about the vein. I had seen enough to realize a fortune in gold was there for the taking. But I had also seen my friend die and I wasn't hankering to share his fate."

"You were afraid to come back."

Gore colored slightly. "To my shame, yes. I was afraid. When our trapping company was disbanded, I went east. I tried to forget about the gold but it proved impossible. The memory ate at me like a cancer. Some nights it was so bad, I'd break out in a sweat." He paused and said softly. "All these years."

"What finally gave you the courage to do it?"

"I looked in the mirror one day and realized I wasn't getting any younger. I'd wasted my life at a common job when I could have lived a life of ease. Right then I made up my mind to do what I should have done long ago."

"And here you are."

"Yes. But I nearly starved crossing the prairie. And when I reached the mountains, I lost my way a couple of times. Finally I reached Fort Bridger, and that's when everything fell into place."

"How?" Fargo asked when Gore didn't go on.

"I ran into Rinson and his men. They would kill their own mothers if there was money to be made. With their help, I realized I could get in and out of Nez Perce country. But it meant sharing the gold. I was reluctant to do that at first. Then the Winston party showed up, and I took it as an omen."

"You've lost me."

"I needed a way to transport the gold. I didn't have the money to buy enough pack animals." Gore grinned. "Their wagons will do quite nicely, don't you think?"

"You son of a bitch."

"All my talk about the valley was for the purpose of luring them here. And they fell for it, the gullible fools. As soon as the vein is picked clean, we'll load the ore on the wagons and be on our way. Simple, eh?"

"And the farmers? What about them?"

"Why, they will be wiped out by the Nez Perce, of course." Gore winked. "Even if the Nez Perce don't do the actual wiping."

"You have it all worked out."

"Don't I, though?" Gore laughed. "The only loose end was you, and now I have you tied up." He laughed louder.

Fargo had to think of something and he had to think of it fast. At any moment Gore could decide to put that bullet in his brain. He still had the Arkansas toothpick in his boot, but it would take time to work the rope loose enough to get at it. Time he didn't have. So he did the only thing he could think of. "All this trouble you've gone to, and all for nothing."

"Eh?" Victor Gore tilted his head. "What are you talking about?"

"The Nez Perce."

"What about them?"

"A war party spotted me about a mile from here. I was running from them when I came across this canyon."

"You're lying."

Fargo shrugged. "You'll find out soon enough." He gazed up at the high canyon walls. "They could be looking down on us even now."

"You're lying, I say."

"I call it fitting that you come back after all these years only to end up like your friend."

Victor Gore stood. Nervously fingering his derringer, he called out, "Mr. Stern, get over here."

Stern came on the run. "What is it?"

"When you were up on the rim did you see any sign of the Nez Perce? Any sign at all?"

"Don't you reckon I'd have told you if I did?"

Gore swung on him, balling his free hand into a fist. "Don't take that tone with me. Did you or didn't you?"

"Hell, no," Stern said. "But I wasn't really looking. I had my eyes on him." Stern jerked a thumb at Fargo.

"I want you to take Larson and go back up. Scour the countryside for sign of the hostiles. And be thorough." Gore glared at Fargo as Stern ran off. "God help you if this is a trick. I'll have Slag stake you out and we'll sit around and watch Perkins go to work on you with his knife. He's vicious, that one. He likes to cut and carve on people."

Fargo didn't respond. His bluff had bought him precious minutes of life and now he had to make the most of them. But what could he do with Gore and the others right there? The ring of picks was continuous. "There's something else you've overlooked."

"Make it good," Gore said skeptically.

"You were right about the army. They did send me. And when I don't report back, patrols will be sent to look for me."

"They won't have troops come this far in. It would provoke a war."

"Keep thinking that," Fargo said. "I'll visit you in the stockade."

Gore drew back a leg as if to kick him but lowered it again. "My interest in you is wearing thin. Were I you, I'd keep quiet."

Fargo took the advice. He'd planted seeds of doubt. Now he must get free. If they let him live until dark, he stood a chance of cutting himself loose. But that was a big "if."

Only a few minutes went by when Stern and Larson came sprinting back around the bend. Stern let out a yell that brought the work to a stop as everyone gathered around to hear what he had to say.

"Smoke! We saw smoke!"

"Calm down," Gore snapped. "Where did you see it? From the direction of the valley?"

"No. North of us, not south. It's not the settlers."

"Injuns," someone said. "We're in for it now."

Most started to talk all at once and Gore silenced them with an angry roar. "A man can't think with all this damn jabbering!" He rubbed his white hair, thinking. "Indians wouldn't make camp this early. For that matter, whites wouldn't, either."

"A village, maybe," Rinson said.

"Lordy, I hope not," Larson said. "If they find us, we'll be up to our ears in redskins."

"Stay calm," Gore stressed. "It could be an army patrol. Fargo, here, might be working with them. The only sure way to find out is to go see. Mr. Rinson, take Perkins and Slag and do just that."

"Why us?" Perkins said. "Why not Stern or Larson or some of the others?"

"Because I picked you," Victor Gore said ominously. "And I don't like being challenged."

Slag said, "I don't mind going. It beats digging out ore."

They ignored Fargo. He tried working his wrists back and forth to create slack but the rope was too tight. Arching his back, he slid his hands to his boots and pried at the knots. They wouldn't give. He was so intent on freeing himself that he didn't hear someone come over. But he saw the shadow that fell across him and felt excruciating pain in his ribs.

"What did I tell you?" Victor Gore said. "I should kill you where you lie but I might have need of you."

Grimacing, Fargo spat out, "Oh?"

"On the off chance you were telling the truth. The army won't dare do anything so long as I have you."

"Use me as a hostage? It won't work."

"You place too little value on your hide. You're a

famous scout. They won't want anything to happen to you." Gore walked off.

Fargo eased onto his other side to spare his aching ribs. He hated to admit it, but he was helpless. All he could do was lie there. The minutes dragged and became hours.

Gore hadn't forgotten about him. Every so often, he glanced over.

His ear to the ground, Fargo heard the rumble of hooves before anyone else. Perkins, alone, came flying back up the canyon and vaulted from his mount before the animal came to a stop. "It's not the army! It's Injuns! Rinson and Slag are keeping an eye on them while I came back to let you know."

"Are they Nez Perce?" Victor Gore asked.

"Hell, I wouldn't know a Nez Perce from a Blackfoot. One redskin looks pretty much the same as any other."

"How many? And more to the point, were they wearing war paint?"

"I should say they were," Perkins confirmed. "I counted seventeen but I might have missed a few."

"How far off are they?"

"A mile, maybe a mile and a half. They were holding some kind of powwow."

"Damn," Gore said. "This complicates things. But we needn't pull out. Not until we have every last ounce of gold."

"We're taking an awful chance," Larson said.

Gore gestured at the burlap sacks. "But well worth it. Or would you rather spend the rest of your life miserably poor?" He began to pace. "At the rate we're digging, if we stick at it all day and all night, we should have most of the gold out by tomorrow morning. Agreed?"

Someone said, "Yes."

"Then all we need to do is keep the war party busy until then. Once we've loaded the gold on the wagons and disposed of the farmers, we can hightail it out of here."

"By 'busy' you mean attack them?" Stern asked.

"Are you insane? No. I aim to distract them another way." Gore glanced at Fargo, and grinned. "Yes, sir. I believe we can give them something to do that will keep them out of our hair. We'll give them a gift, as it were."

Fargo didn't like the sound of that.

"I don't savvy," Larson said.

"You will."

Gore crooked a finger at Perkins and they moved out of earshot. Whatever Gore said made Perkins cackle. As Perkins ran up the canyon to do Gore's bidding, Gore came back, and hunkered.

"This will be our last talk. I want to thank you for showing up when you did. And for telling me about the war party you saw."

"I didn't see one," Fargo confessed.

Gore laughed and slapped his thigh. "Then the joke's on you, isn't it? How fitting. The army will never learn what became of you. All they will know is that you rode off into the wilds to do their bidding and were never heard from again." He chuckled. "Any kin you want me to send word to?"

"Your true nature is showing."

"I have put on a bit of an act, haven't I? And I've done quite well, if I do say so myself."

Fargo almost told him he had lied about the army, too. "You're not out of the woods yet."

"True," Gore agreed. "Every moment we stay, we're in mortal peril. But my prospects are a lot rosier than yours."

"You're really going to do it? Kill all those women and children?"

"What are they to me? It's no different than drowning a litter of puppies you don't want."

"You hide it well," Fargo said.

Gore sobered, and frowned. "Save your insults. None of us are perfect. Except for Martha Winston." He snickered.

"When your turn comes I hope you die screaming."

"Now, now. Is that any way to talk to someone who has arranged a special surprise for you?"

"What kind of surprise?"

"Let me put it this way." Victor Gore glowed with sadistic glee. "You'll die screaming a lot sooner than I will."

17

"This spot will do," Rinson said.

Draped belly down over a horse, Fargo could see gray tendrils rising from the forest canopy half a mile away. Jostled by the ride, his side sore from rubbing against the saddle horn, he didn't pay attention when the others dismounted and paid for his neglect when rough hands seized his legs and upended him. He tried to absorb the force of the fall by twisting so he hit with his shoulders but he only partially succeeded. A kick compounded the pain.

"That was for all the trouble you've caused us," Perkins said gleefully.

Slag chuckled. "Kick him again. Kick him so hard, you stave his ribs in."

"None of that," Rinson said. "We need him alive to keep the redskins busy, remember?"

"A few busted ribs won't kill him," Slag said. "He'll still be breathing when they find him."

"No," Rinson snapped. "Gore told us how he wants it done and that's how we'll do it."

Perkins remarked, "I can't get over how you let him boss us around."

"He didn't have to cut us in but he did. For that we should be grateful."

"More for us if he's worm food."

"God, you're a greedy bastard," Rinson said. "And in case you've forgotten, I gave my word and shook on it."

"Since when does that count? We've always looked

127

out for us and no one else. If you ask me, we don't owe Gore a thing."

"I didn't ask you. Now get to gathering the firewood so we can get the hell out of here."

Fargo was perplexed. It was foolhardy to make a fire so close to the war party. But Slag and Perkins hurried into the trees and shortly returned with their arms laden with broken limbs and kindling. They heaped it in a pile, and Slag rummaged in his saddlebags and produced a fire steel and flint.

"Any last words?" Rinson taunted.

"I expect to be around a good long while yet."

"Do you, now?" Rinson laughed. "Bold talk for an hombre who won't see the dawn." He slowly drew his Remington and just as slowly thumbed back the hammer. "Are you sure you don't have any last words?"

"You wouldn't let Perkins bust my ribs but you're fixing to shoot me?" Fargo shook his head. "I doubt it."

Rinson waggled the Remington. "Oh, this isn't for you."

Slag was puffing lightly on a tiny flame so it would grow.

"I wish we could see what they do to him," Perkins said. "I saw a soldier once after the Sioux got done with him. The things they did you wouldn't believe. It must have taken him hours to die."

"You almost sound as if you admire them," Rinson said.

"I admire anyone who is good at what they do. And when it comes to carving on people, redskins have us whites beat all hollow."

Slag stopped puffing. "I've said it before and I'll say it now. You're not right in your head."

The flames were spreading. Smoke coiled up into the sky, growing thicker by the moment.

"I get it," Fargo said. "You're hoping the war party will spot the smoke and come find me."

"Oh, they'll spot it, all right," Rinson said. Raising the Remington, he fired three shots into the air, one right after the other. "We're close enough; they're bound to hear that."

Pleased with themselves, the three cutthroats climbed on their mounts and reined around. Rinson gave a little wave. "I'll think of them cutting on you while I'm having my way with that filly you've been poking."

They cackled and were gone.

Bending his back into a bow, Fargo sought to slide his fingers into his boot. The rope thwarted him. He pried at the knot, pried so hard he thought his fingernails would tear off, to no avail.

Every second counted. The warriors were bound to have seen the smoke by now. They would come on warily, though, suspicious of a trick, and that would slow them some.

Fargo figured he had five minutes, if that. There was no way in hell he could free himself before the warriors got there. They would find him bound and helpless, exactly as Victor Gore wanted.

Crackling from the fire sparked an idea.

Quickly turning so his back was to the flames, Fargo wriggled backward. The heat was excruciating, and got worse. Gritting his teeth, he looked over his shoulder and thrust his wrists into the fire. He tried to burn the rope and only the rope but it was impossible. His sleeves were soon ablaze, and the smell of his burning flesh filled the air. He stood it as long as he could. Then, uttering a low groan, he jerked his arms from the flames and rolled back and forth on his back to smother them.

Bunching his shoulders, Fargo exerted all his strength. But all he succeeded in doing was dig the rope deeper into his wrists. He tried again, exerting every sinew in his arms and shoulders, and felt himself grow red in the face. But once again the rope refused to break.

Fargo was sure the flames had weakened it. Again his muscles bulged. If he failed this time, he would stick his boots in the fire and try to burn the rope around his ankles before his feet were charred and useless.

A *snap* threw Fargo off balance. Although his hands

and wrists were welters of pain, he rolled over and set to work on his ankles. Untying the knots now was easy.

Fargo started to stand. A whinny off in the underbrush warned him the warriors were almost there.

Fargo ran. He made it into the woods and threw himself to the ground just as the first warrior appeared—a Nez Perce with a bow, an arrow nocked. The warrior drew rein and gazed about. Presently he was joined by others, until fully twenty painted warriors were trying to make sense of the shots and the untended fire.

Fargo reckoned they would spread out and search for sign. In which case they were bound to find the tracks of the shod horses, and would follow them to the canyon. But to his consternation, the warriors just sat there, talking. Not one climbed down to examine the ground.

Then another Nez Perce arrived. Why he came so late, Fargo couldn't say. But it was Winter Wolf. The others stopped talking and patiently waited while the old warrior did what they should have done. Dismounting, Winter Wolf walked in ever widening circles, his aged form bent. Finally he said something that excited the rest.

Fargo wished he could see the expression on Victor Gore's face when the Nez Perce blocked the mouth of the canyon and fired down on the white invaders from the canyon rim. The whites had rifles but the Indians had numbers.

Winter Wolf straightened. He spoke and the others listened. His horse was brought. Raising an arm, he uttered a sharp cry and led the war party in the direction Rinson, Perkins and Slag had gone.

Fargo smiled. It would serve Victor Gore and the so-called protectors right if they were wiped out.

When the last of the Nez Perce had melted into the greenery, Fargo cautiously stood. Only when he was convinced they were gone did he walk to the fire. What now? he wondered. He was unarmed and on foot and miles from the valley and the settlers. He broke into a jog.

The swatch of broken undergrowth made by the Nez Perce enabled Fargo to travel faster than he otherwise could. He prided himself on his ability to run long distances without tiring, and now that ability was put to the test.

Fargo was about halfway to the canyon when the unexpected occurred. The trail veered to the east. His first thought was that Rinson realized they were being chased and sought to lead the war party away from Gore and the gold. But as Fargo moved about reading sign, he discovered a track that changed his thinking. It was a human footprint. A boot print. He soon found others. Three sets, in all. And all three pointed toward the canyon.

It wasn't hard to figure out. Rinson, Perkins and Slag had dismounted and given their animals slaps on the rump. Then they set out on foot for the canyon. The Nez Perce, eager to overtake them, saw where the horse tracks led on east and didn't bother to stop. The warriors were chasing riderless mounts.

Fargo pushed on. When he was within sight of the canyon, he drew back into the trees and hurried to where he had left the Ovaro. Shock stopped him dead in midstride.

The pinto was gone.

Once again Fargo searched for sign. He worried that the Nez Perce were to blame, in which case recovering the pinto might prove impossible. But no, boot prints showed where a white man had led the stallion off.

But now a new mystery presented itself.

Fargo figured one of Gore's men found it and took it into the canyon. But no. The tracks led *away*. Fargo followed them and came to a spot where another man and two horses had been waiting. The pair climbed on and rode off, taking the Ovaro with them.

"What the hell?" Fargo said out loud. If Gore and his men weren't to blame, then who was?

Fargo could push on after the pinto, or he could pay

Gore and company a visit and help himself to one of their animals. He liked that idea, and bent his steps toward the canyon.

A mount wasn't his only reason. They had taken his Colt and Henry, and he wanted the rifle and six-shooter back. Some might argue that one gun was as good as any other, but that wasn't true. When a man was used to a gun, it became part of him. He was better with it than with any other. Fargo had used his Colt for so long, he would feel awkward using any other.

Giving the mouth of the canyon a wide berth, Fargo started up the slope. No one was keeping watch, which surprised him.

Learning from his mistake, Fargo was alert for a sentry at the top. But this time no one was there.

Worming from boulder to boulder, Fargo smiled when the peal of metal on rock confirmed they were still hard at work. Removing his hat, he risked a peek. They were all there, including Rinson, Perkins and Slag.

Fargo remembered Gore saying they'd work all night. That gave him hours to spare. He would wait until dark, then sneak down. He made special note of who had his Henry—it was Stern—and who had his Colt—none other than Victor Gore.

Grateful for the chance to rest, Fargo used his arm for a pillow and closed his eyes. He was battered and sore and his ribs wouldn't stop hurting. He intended to lie there a bit and then keep watch until sunset. But the next thing he knew, he opened his eyes and the stars were out.

Fargo bit off a few choice words. He had fallen asleep. Mad at himself, he wedged his hat on and inched to the edge for another look. A fire blazed at the bottom of the canyon. Clustered around it were the old trapper and his gold hounds. They had stopped work to eat supper. Judging by their smiles and mirth, they were having a fine time. In a couple of months they would be back in civilization, as rich as could be.

But not if Fargo could help it.

Turning, he crawled until he was near the bottom, then rose and stealthily descended to the valley floor. The smart thing was to wait until most of them were asleep but since they planned to stay up all night, what good would it do?

Fargo couldn't stop thinking of the settlers and the danger they were in. He must warn them. He snuck to the bend and peeked past it.

Gore and his hirelings were about done eating. Wood was added to the fire, and soon they were at the vein, their picks and shovels flailing, their shadows flicking on the rock wall.

The horses were picketed between Fargo and the vein. Easing down, he crabbed toward them, careful to stay close to the wall. Whenever one of the cutthroats so much as raised his head, Fargo froze. Only Slag glanced in his direction; but Slag was mopping his sweaty brow with a sleeve.

Several of the horses realized Fargo was there. But the trapper and the gun sharks were so intent on the gold, they didn't catch on.

His confidence climbing, Fargo crawled faster. He was almost to the first horse when it stamped and whinnied. Amazingly, once again no one paid attention.

Gold had that effect. It dazzled the mind. It made men forget themselves and think only of the riches the gold would bring. Perkins, in fact, was holding a lump of gold-laced quartz in the palm of his hand and running his fingers over it as if caressing a lover.

The horses had been picketed to prevent them from running off. But it was the work of an instant for Fargo to slash the first rope with his Arkansas toothpick. He moved to the next animal, and then the third. He had cut four of them loose when Victor Gore unexpectedly straightened.

"We're making good time, boys. By morning we'll have the gold ready to load on the wagons."

"You did say we're not to leave a single settler breathing, right?" Perkins asked.

"Do you disagree?"

"Hell, no." Perkins laughed. "I've never had a problem killing folks. Or anything else."

Gore turned. "Mr. Larson, would you be so kind as to fetch more burlap bags."

"Right away." Larson nodded and hustled toward the horse string.

Fargo tensed. The bags must be bundled on one of the horses, but which one? He couldn't tell from where he was lying. He hoped it was a horse at the other end.

Larson came almost straight toward him. Fortunately, he was staring at the ground. Then, when only a few feet away, he glanced up—and stopped in his tracks.

"Mr. Gore! Rinson! It's Fargo! He's here!"

18

Larson should have gone for his six-shooter. His shout bought Fargo the split second he needed to surge to his feet, the toothpick low at his side. Larson's hand swooped to his revolver but by then Fargo was next to him. The razor-sharp double-edged blade lanced up and in. Larson gasped and stiffened and was dead on his feet.

There were bellows of outrage and fiery oaths from the others. Then, almost as one, they clawed for their own hardware.

Fargo snatched Larson's revolver. It was a Smith & Wesson. The barrel was longer than his Colt's and the grips were different but the caliber was the same. It bucked when he squeezed off a shot and the nearest man clutched at his chest and crumpled.

Whirling, Fargo ran to one of the horses he had cut loose. The shot and the shouts had spooked it and it was turning down the canyon. A bound brought him alongside.

As six-guns boomed and lead buzzed, Fargo leaped, caught hold of the saddle horn, and swung astride the saddle. A hard jab of his spurs brought the animal to a gallop. Swinging onto the side, Comanche fashion, he raced toward the bend. His skin crawled with the expectation of taking a slug but he wasn't hit.

"After him!" Victor Gore roared. "Don't let him get away!"

In a thunder of hooves Fargo was around the bend and momentarily safe. Swinging back up, he rode for his life. He wished he had the Ovaro under him. The horse under him was fast but not as fast as his stallion.

In no time Fargo was out of the canyon and flew into the trees. Bringing the horse to a stop, he looked back.

Riders swept out of the canyon in pursuit. When they didn't spot him, they drew rein.

"Which way did he go?" one shouted. It sounded like Stern.

"Shut up and we can hear him!" Rinson snapped.

Fargo patted his horse to keep it still.

"I don't hear anything," Slag hollered.

Perkins' voice rose. "I bet he's making for the dirt-pushers. He'll warn them we'll be coming for their wagons."

"Let him!" Rinson said, and uttered a hard laugh. "Do you honestly think they'll believe him? They trust us, remember."

"What do we do, then?" Slag asked.

"We go back and get the rest of the gold out," Rinson said. "Come morning, we'll be ready for the wagons, just like Gore wants."

Fargo stayed where he was until they filed into the canyon. Then he raised the reins. His natural impulse was to fly through the woods to reach the valley as soon as possible but it was dark and the war party was out there, somewhere.

It seemed to take forever.

A lone campfire in the center of the circled wagons served as a beacon. No one challenged him as he rode up.

Passing between two of the covered wagons, Fargo wearily drew rein. Sleeping forms were all around. The saddle creaked as he stiffly climbed down.

The guard didn't appear.

Fargo reckoned the man Rinson had left behind must be sleeping. He quietly stole to a row of figures next to the Winstons' wagon. The largest was snoring loud enough to cause an earthquake. Dropping to one knee, Fargo shook his shoulder.

"Lester, wake up."

The big farmer snorted and muttered and went on sleeping.

"Lester, damn it." Fargo shook harder and this time Lester rolled onto his back and his eyes blinked a few times.

"What? Who? What time is it?"

The position of the Big Dipper gave Fargo some idea. "About one in the morning. You need to get up. You have trouble on the way."

Rubbing his face, Lester sluggishly rose onto his elbows. "What are you talking about? What kind of trouble?"

"Gore and Rinson are coming here to wipe your people out."

Lester stopped rubbing. "Say that again? I must be befuddled by sleep. Or else I'm dreaming."

"Gore and Rinson aim to kill all of you."

"All of us?"

"I know I sound loco but I'm serious, damn it. Gore has found gold. He needs a way to transport it out. So he's taking your wagons."

For fully half a minute the farmer simply stared. Then he cleared his throat and said, "I've had a hard day and need my sleep."

Exasperation made Fargo boil. "Damn you, listen to me. Gore didn't come back to this part of the country just to see it again. He was after the gold all along. He found a vein back when he was a trapper and now he needs your wagons to get the ore out."

"You don't say," Lester said. "But if Victor found gold that long ago, why did he wait all this time to come back for it?"

"He didn't want his scalp lifted."

Lester smiled a tolerant smile. "Let me get back to sleep and we'll talk about this in the morning."

"They'll be on their way by then."

"And take how long to get here?"

"If they start at sunrise they can be here by midmorning."

"Then we have plenty of time, don't we?" Lester started to lie back down but Fargo gripped his wrist.

"Why won't you believe me?"

"I didn't say I didn't. I didn't say I do. But if I understand you, you're saying that Gore tricked us into coming to this valley. You're forgetting that I was the one who insisted we come. Victor tried to talk me out of it." Lester gave a strange sort of laugh.

"He's clever," Fargo said. "He got you to think it was your idea when it was his doing all along."

"No, it wasn't."

"Please," Fargo said. "Don't do this."

"Let me sleep." Lester sank back down. "I'm plumb worn-out and can't think straight."

"But Gore and Rinso—" Fargo began.

"We'll talk in the morning." Lester rolled onto his side so his back was to him. "I'll listen to whatever else you have to say then."

Fargo's anger turned to fury. He had gone through a lot to warn them, and now the lunkhead wouldn't listen. Then again, he could understand why Lester thought his story was far-fetched. How could he convince him? he wondered. The answer was like a slap in the face. He shook Winston's shoulder again.

"You're becoming a nuisance."

"The man Rinson left to guard you. Where is he?"

"We don't know. He rode off shortly before sunset. Said he saw some riders in the trees. He never came back."

"And you didn't send anyone to look for him?"

With an exaggerated sigh, Lester rolled onto his back. "Of course we did. I went myself, with some others. But there was no sign of him. We planned to search again once the sun is up."

Fargo glanced at the ring of covered wagons. "So who is standing guard tonight?"

"We're taking turns. I believe Floyd should be on watch. But it's been so quiet, it wouldn't surprise me if he fell asleep." Lester rolled over once more. "I'd very much like to do the same. Good night."

Fargo checked an impulse to swear a mean streak. He rose and tied the horse to the rear wheel.

Suddenly a warm hand closed on his wrist and warm breath fanned his ear. "Welcome back, handsome. Did you miss me?" Rachel whispered.

"Didn't you hear what I just told your father?"

"Sure I did. But we have the rest of the night and everyone is asleep." Giggling softly, Rachel tugged on his arm. "Come on. Let's go for a stroll."

Fargo couldn't believe it. These people had blocks of wood for brains. Here he was, trying to save their hides, and they treated him as if he were a simpleton.

"Come on," Rachel said again, pulling.

Fargo let her usher him around to the other side of their wagon. There she stopped and gazed off toward the timber.

"If we hurry, we can be back in an hour or so."

"You don't care that Gore and Rinson aim to kill all of you?"

"Not until the middle of the morning. Your very own words." Rachel grinned and took a step.

Fargo shook his head in bewilderment. Now was hardly the right time. Then again, everyone else *was* asleep, and Gore and Rinson wouldn't be there for eight or nine hours yet. "Why go anywhere?" he whispered, and didn't budge.

Rachel regarded him uncertainly. "Then where?"

Turning her so her back was to the wagon, Fargo pressed her against it. His hands on her hips, his mouth close to hers, he said, "Right here."

"They'll hear us."

"Not if we're quiet." Fargo kissed her. She tensed, then gradually relaxed. Her mouth parted and their tongues met in a wet, silken swirl. She started to groan but caught herself.

"That was nice," Rachel whispered when they drew apart. "I think about you doing that all the time."

"Do you ever think about this?" Fargo asked. Cupping both her breasts over the long cotton nightgown she wore, he squeezed them as if they were ripe melons.

Gasping, Rachel arched her back, her body taut against him, her thighs flush with his. "Oh, God."

"Careful," Fargo said with a grin. "You don't want to wake them." Her nipples become tacks and he pinched them between his thumbs and forefingers. It elicited a tiny mew. Her fingernails sank into his shoulders.

"The things you do to me," Rachel husked. "No man has ever made me tingle like you do."

Fargo silenced her with another kiss. She ground her hips against him, her twin peaks mashed against his chest, her fingers exploring high and low. She caressed his legs but didn't touch him *there* just yet. When he ran his tongue from her mouth to her chin and then to the soft curve of her neck, she shivered.

"I could do this all night."

Not Fargo. He wanted to get it over with so he could catch some sleep. But there was no rush. He licked her neck. He nibbled on her ear. For her part, she kissed his forehead, then took off his hat, dropped it, and ran her hand through his hair.

Rachel dreamily whispered in his ear, "You know, if things work out, you'll be the second-best part of this whole business."

Idly wondering what she meant, Fargo delved his tongue under the top of her nightgown as low as it would go. He couldn't reach her nipples so he started to hike up her nightgown.

Rachel gripped his wrists. "I don't know. Maybe we shouldn't."

"You started this," Fargo reminded her. Swatting her hand away, he yanked her nightgown up and plunged his hand underneath. At the contact of his fingers with her thighs, her mouth became a delectable oval of raw desire. She kissed him fiercely, her passion uncontrollable.

Sculpting her smooth skin as if it were warm clay, Fargo kneaded her thighs, starting at her knees and kneading upward. She grew warmer, and her ardor climbed. She thrust hard against him, rubbing herself on his iron member. When he lightly brushed her nether region, she bit his shoulder, then whispered excitedly into his ear.

"Yes! Yes! Do me! Do me right here!"

Fargo wasn't about to stop. Spreading her legs, he pried at his belt and pants. When his pole was free, he ran the tip along her moist slit. Her reaction was to rise up onto her toes and practically bury her nails in his upper arms. The pain distracted him a few moments, and the next he knew, she had a hand down there and was fondling him.

"You're magnificent. Do you know that?"

"Not so loud," Fargo warned. The last thing he needed was to wake her mother and have Martha come charging around the wagon with a cleaver or an ax.

"I want you in me," Rachel breathed into his ear. "And don't worry. I'll keep quiet."

Fargo thought he heard a sound, and paused.

"What are you waiting for?" Rachel impatiently whispered.

Before Fargo could reply, she rose higher, shifted slightly, and impaled her exquisite rose on his engorged thorn.

Sucking in a deep breath, Rachel closed her eyes and rested her forehead on his chin. "You have no idea how good that feels."

"Care to bet?" The very first time Fargo coupled with a woman, he became addicted. To him, the soft savor of a female body in the throes of lust was as good as life got. He could never get enough.

"Don't stand there like a fence post," Rachel teased. "Do something, will you?"

"Whatever the lady wants."

"Read my mind."

Giving her no chance to set herself, Fargo rammed up into her. Rachel threw her head back and bit her lower lip to keep from crying out. Then it was more of the same, up and in, up and in, in an ever faster tempo, Fargo rising onto the tips of his toes with each penetration.

Rachel was in a delirium of rapture, her eyelids hooded, her mouth forming soundless cries as she matched him stroke for stroke.

The explosion ripped Fargo out of himself and left him near breathless with pleasure. Luxuriating in the feeling, he sagged against Rachel and felt her fingers at the nape of his neck.

"I'm sorry," Rachel said.

Not sure he had heard her correctly, Fargo responded, "What do you have to be sorry about?"

Rachel Winston wistfully smiled and tenderly ran a finger along his jaw. "If you only knew."

19

Pink and gold tinged the eastern sky when Lester Winston grunted and sat up. Scratching himself, he sleepily regarded the slumbering figures on either side of him. He looked up and gave a slight start. "My word. You shouldn't scare people like that."

Fargo had been up for half an hour. He had failed to make his point before, but he would by God make it now. "Do you remember what I told you last night?"

"How could I forget?"

"We need to talk about it some more."

"Can't it wait until I've had my coffee?" Lester asked, running his big fingers through his hair. "I'm not hardly awake yet."

"You're awake enough. The lives of your family and all your friends are at stake."

"It won't be like you think it will."

"Damn it, Lester. Don't do this. You're in danger. You and everyone here. Gore really found gold. He needs your wagons to transport it out of Nez Perce country, and he will have them, by God, even if it means wiping all of you out."

Lester chuckled. "Did I ask you if you had been drinking?"

Fargo almost hit him. "What does it take to get something through that thick skull of yours?"

"Calm down."

"The hell I will," Fargo fumed. "I've never met anyone so pigheaded in all my life."

"There is no need for insults. I wish you could put yourself in my boots. Then you wouldn't be so mad."

Fargo grabbed him by the front of his shirt. "You must warn everyone. You must arm them and be ready when Gore and his killers ride in."

"When Victor and our protectors ride in," Lester corrected him.

Fargo drew back. "To hell with you. I'll warn the others myself so they can defend themselves."

"You'll do no such thing. These are my people." The big farmer smiled. "Now please. Calm yourself. Trust me when I say all will be well. The Good Lord has watched over us from the start and He won't forsake us now."

"Damn you." If beating sense into Winston would do any good, Fargo would gladly pound him to a pulp. "You're asking for an early grave."

"If you only knew," Lester said.

Fargo remembered Rachel saying the exact same thing. He was about to ask what Lester meant when merry chortling let him know someone else was awake.

"He sure is funny, Pa," Billy said. "He looks fit to lay an egg."

"Be nice, boy," the father chided. "He's worried about us, is all. That's to his credit."

"He's worried about Sis," Billy said.

Lester made Fargo madder by laughing. "No doubt that's true. But we should still be nice to him."

Fargo quickly said, "Then you'll warn the rest? You'll be ready for Gore when he rides in?"

"I'm curious. Ready how, exactly? Do you expect us to shoot them from their saddles?"

Billy laughed.

Fargo walked away. It was either that or slug Lester. He went around to the other side of the wagon to cool down. He reminded himself he still had time to warn the settlers himself.

The morning routine got under way.

Rachel gave Fargo a warm smile upon awakening. She

144

languidly stretched, her breasts swelling against her nightgown, and showed the pink tip of her tongue between her lips so only he could see. "Good morning, handsome."

Martha bustled about preparing breakfast. So did other women.

The men gathered in the middle of the circle for their morning talk about what they planned to do that day.

Fargo got their attention by raising his arms. "I have something to say to you."

All eyes swung toward him, and then to Lester Winston, who frowned and sighed.

"I suppose we have no choice but to hear him out. He won't let it drop otherwise."

"I sure won't," Fargo confirmed. "I've tried to warn your leader but he has no more sense than a goat. Victor Gore is coming to kill you."

No one said anything.

"Didn't you hear me? Gore and Rinson are in cahoots. They need your wagons to take gold back to civilization."

All they did was stare until one farmer said to Winston, "This is what he's so agitated about?"

That was the last straw. Fargo shouldered in among them, growling, "What the hell is the matter with you people? You have families. Wives and kids. Don't you care that they could all be dead soon?"

"That won't happen," a farmer declared.

"We love our families," yet another said.

"I don't see you rushing for your guns," Fargo told them. "You don't even act like you believe me."

"We're tillers of the soil, not killers," the one named Harvey said.

"You're idiots, is what you are," Fargo said gruffly. "Plain, goddamned, stupid as hell idiots."

Lester wagged a thick finger. "That will be enough of that kind of talk. I won't have you insulting us."

"Then listen to me, damn it," Fargo said in baffled outrage. "I've done all I can and you ignore me."

145

"Now, now," Lester Winston said, as he might to Billy if his son were misbehaving. "We appreciate it. We truly do. But the best thing now is for all of us to relax and eat our breakfasts. You should do the same. A hot meal is always good for the disposition."

Fargo gestured in disgust. "I wash my hands of the whole bunch of you. If you're massacred, you have only yourself to blame."

"We won't be harmed," Harvey confidently replied.

"We trust in providence, friend," another said, and many of them bobbed their heads.

Fargo left them and went over to the Winstons' wagon. He was so mad he smacked the side.

"Keep that up and you'll hurt your hand." Rachel, fully dressed, her hair in a bonnet, was next to him. "What's gotten into you?"

Fargo related his attempt to convince her father and the other men to take up arms. He clutched her. "You must talk to them. Persuade them to get ready for Gore. It's their only hope."

"I trust my pa to do what's best."

"But he has wax in his ears."

Just then Martha announced that the coffee was ready. He went to the fire. "What about you, Mrs. Winston? You must have heard me talking to your husband."

"About Victor Gore? Yes."

"Then do something. Get the men to take up arms, and have the women and the children take cover."

"And then what?" Martha asked. "Blast Mr. Gore and Mr. Rinson to kingdom come as they ride up?"

"If you want to go on breathing."

Martha shook the large wooden spoon she had been using to stir oatmeal. "Shame on you. You've lived on the frontier too long. You hold human life much too cheaply."

"Don't you care if you live or die?"

"Of course," Martha replied. "But I didn't agree with them and I don't agree with you. We're not beasts.

Scripture says we're made in His image. 'Thou shalt not kill' comes straight from His mouth."

"Gore doesn't share your sentiments. All he cares about is the gold and getting it back East." Fargo stopped. "Wait. What was that about agreeing?"

"I'm against taking human life. A white life, at any rate."

"Indians don't count, huh?"

"They don't believe in the one true God. They don't live by the Ten Commandments. I doubt they even have souls. Killing a red savage is the same as killing a fish or a squirrel."

Fargo never did like those who wore their bigotry on their sleeve. Or in this case, on their dress. "You make me sorry I'm trying to help."

Martha dipped the spoon in the pot. "The Lord works in mysterious ways, His wonders to perform."

"What does that have to do with anything?"

"You'll find out soon enough. When you do, don't hold it against me."

"I don't have the slightest notion what in hell you're talking about," Fargo informed her. He thought she would explain but she went on moving the spoon in small circles.

The next moment Billy came up, gave him a peculiar look, and snickered. "I heard what you just told my ma. You sure are dumb, mister."

"William!" Martha turned. "None of that, you hear? He's not like we are. He doesn't realize how hard this is for us."

"It's not hard for me," the boy said.

"Go help your pa with the wagons. We want to be ready when the time comes."

"You're going somewhere?" Fargo asked.

"No."

Fed up, Fargo wheeled. His gaze drifted to the rope corral and for a second he thought he was seeing things. "My horse!" he blurted.

"How's that?" Martha said, her attention on the oatmeal.

"How did my horse get here?"

"Oh. Lester brought it in. Seems he found your animal tied to a tree somewhere and you were nowhere around."

Fargo was halfway to the rope corral when it hit him. He had left the Ovaro in the woods near the canyon. If Lester had been there, then Lester must know where Gore was. But why hadn't Lester said anything? He pushed down on the rope and stepped over. As he was patting the stallion's neck someone coughed to get his attention.

It was Lester. He was holding a shotgun. And Lester was pointing the shotgun at him. Harvey and another farmer flanked Lester, both with rifles. "I'll have to ask you to come out of there and over to my wagon."

"What the hell is this?"

"I must insist," Lester said. "It's for your own good. Harvey, here, will relieve you of that six-shooter. Then if you do as we say, there won't be any trouble."

"Don't," Fargo said.

"It's for your own good." Lester motioned with the shotgun. "I don't have a lot of time to argue. Victor and Mr. Rinson might be here sooner than we think, and we don't want you to cause trouble for us."

"Damn you."

"I'm sorry. I truly am. But you're too headstrong. I'm afraid Gore will come riding in and you'll put lead into him before he can open his mouth."

"It would be best for everyone if I did." Fargo doubted Lester would shoot but all it would take was an involuntary twitch of Lester's trigger finger and he would be blown in half. His arms out from his sides, he moved to the rope.

"No tricks, now," Lester warned.

Harvey relieved Fargo of the six-gun and stepped back. The third farmer pushed on the rope so Fargo could step over it. As they crossed the circle, others gathered to watch. Not a shred of sympathy showed on a single face, except Rachel's. She came over as Fargo was forced at shotgun-point to sit with his back to the wheel.

"Must we, Pa?"

"It's for the best."

"But he's our friend."

"You know what's at stake, girl. It can't be helped."

"What can't be helped?" Fargo asked.

No one answered him.

A couple of men came forward with rope and went to tie him to the wheel but Lester intervened. "If Gore and Rinson see him tied up, they'll wonder why. And they can't be the least bit suspicious or it won't work."

Fargo tried again. "What won't work?"

"Tell him," Martha said.

"Not now, dear," Lester replied.

"Tell him. He has a right to know. You've used him as you used those others."

Lester smiled down at Fargo. "She doesn't approve of what we're about to do. Fact is, she's objected from the start."

"The start of *what*, damn it."

"Haven't you figured it out yet?" Lester's voice was thick with pride. "We've known about the gold since Fort Bridger. My son likes to sneak around and listen to people, and he heard Gore and Rinson talking one night. This was before Gore came to me and mentioned the valley."

Fargo was stunned. "You've known all along? Then why did you let them lead you here? Why did you let them use you?"

"You've got it backwards. They didn't use us. *We* used *them*. We played along so they would think we came here to farm. But we're still bound for Oregon. Only now when we get there, each of us will be able to buy more land than we'll know what to do with, and live in a fine house, besides."

Fargo stared at the dozens of faces staring at him, and

what he saw reflected on many of them made him half sick. "Dear God."

"That's right," Lester crowed. "Victor Gore is in for a surprise. He came all this way and went to all that trouble for nothing. We're helping ourselves to the gold. And anyone who tries to stop us is as good as dead."

20

Victor Gore and Rinson and their companions rode into the valley along about ten. They were smiling and friendly and greeted the farmers with "Morning!" and nods. None of them noticed that most of the women were gathered at the opposite end of the circle with the children under their wing, or if they did notice, they thought nothing of it. And none noticed that two burly farmers with rifles stood on either side of Fargo. In fact, all the farmers had rifles and shotguns, and four of the women, besides. One of those women was Rachel.

Lester had the revolver they had taken from Fargo wedged under his belt, covered by his jacket so none of the "protectors" could see it. Spreading his arms, he beamed and said, "Victor! Where have you been? We were getting worried."

Victor Gore tiredly leaned on his saddle horn. "We've been scouring the countryside for those savages. We found where they had camped and tracked them for miles but never could catch up with them."

"That's a shame," Lester said. "If you had thrashed them, it would teach those heathens to leave us be."

"My thinking exactly." Gore straightened and gazed about the circle. His eyes fell on Fargo and he stiffened. "What's this? Where did he come from?"

"He showed up late last night," Lester said. "He tried to feed me some cock-and-bull story. For your sake, I had him disarmed."

"My sake?" Gore repeated.

"He tried to convince me that you are out to harm

us. Can you believe it? I refused to listen to his non-sense. But I was afraid he might shoot you, so I took his six-shooter away from him."

"You did good," Gore complimented him. "And don't worry. Mr. Rinson and I know exactly how to deal with him."

"I thought you might."

Only Fargo seemed to be aware that the farmers and the armed women were slowly and casually drifting closer to the riders, and had them surrounded. Fargo shifted, and a rifle muzzle poked him in the side.

"Keep still," Harvey warned. "It's for your own good."

"It will be a bloodbath," Fargo said quietly. "Is that what you want?"

"We have surprise on our side," Harvey said while grinning to give the impression they were having a friendly talk.

"You're fools."

"Can't you understand how much that gold means to us?" Harvey whispered. "None of us have ever had a chance like this. To have more money than any of us have ever seen. Think of all the things we can do for our families."

"You're not doing it for them. You're doing it for the same reason Gore came back here. For the same reason Gore and Rinson want all of you dead." Fargo paused. "You're doing it for greed."

To his surprise, Harvey bobbed his chin. "Maybe you're right. Maybe that's all there is to it. But do you know what? I don't care. Neither do most of the others. We want that gold and we will have it."

"It won't be of much use to you if you're dead."

"Save your breath. We've come too far to change our minds."

The other farmer nodded in silent agreement.

"God help you," Fargo told them.

Victor Gore was gazing about the circle. "Say. Where's the man I left to stand guard while we were gone?"

"He up and disappeared," Lester replied. "He said something about seeing men off in the woods and went for a look-see. But he never came back."

Only then did Fargo realize the truth—the farmers had killed him.

"What?" Gore blurted. "Didn't you try to find him? Didn't you look for sign?"

"Of course. But it was as if he vanished into thin air. We figured the savages got hold of him and must be close by. That's why we armed ourselves."

Fargo had to hand it to him. The big farmer had it all worked out. And Gore fell for the lie.

"A wise precaution. But now that we're here, you can put your guns down and get back to making this valley your new home." Gore went to slide a boot from the stirrups.

"Not so fast," Lester said, his hand rising from under his jacket with the revolver pointed at Gore's chest.

The next instant all the farmers had their weapons trained on their former protectors. Rinson and the rest stared in disbelief, unsure what was going on or how they should react.

"What is this, Lester?" Victor Gore demanded.

"We'd like for you and your friends to shed your hardware. And we'd like for you to do it nice and slow so we don't have to shoot any more of you."

"Any more?" Gore said, and recoiled as if the big farmer had struck him. "I ask you again. What is the meaning of this?"

"Come now. Don't play the innocent. We know, Victor."

"You know what?" Gore asked. But it was plain from the way he paled that he had divined the truth.

"We know about the gold. We know about your plan to wipe us out and take our wagons. But we can't allow that."

Gore shot Fargo a look of pure hate. "You did this!"

"No, he didn't," Lester Winston said. "It was my Billy. He overheard you and Rinson at Fort Bridger.

153

Boys do that. They like to spy on folks and listen when they shouldn't."

"You've known all this time?"

"I'm afraid so."

"This is bad," Victor Gore said grimly.

"For you, yes," Lester agreed. "But not for us. Thanks to you, all of us will soon be rich. Thanks to you, we can live out the rest of our days in comfort. I thank you."

"Do you really think it will be this easy? That we'll hand the gold over to you just like that?" Gore snapped his fingers.

Lester wagged the revolver. "Look around you. Have your men do as I asked and drop their weapons. If you don't, I'm afraid we'll have to blow every last one of you from your saddles."

"Bastard," Victor said. "You miserable, thieving bastard."

"Now, now. You're a fine one to talk. You planned to murder innocent women and children." Lester extended the revolver and thumbed back the hammer. "I must insist. Do as I tell you or there will be hell to pay."

Fargo tensed. Rinson and his men had no doubt killed before, many times, and they probably figured that a bunch of dirt farmers were no match for them. But greed had made the farmers just like them. Greed had turned the farmers into killers. Blood was about to be spilled. An awful lot of blood.

"It need not come to this," Victor Gore was saying. "I'm willing to share the gold with you and your people. Lower your guns and we will sit down and talk this over."

"I wouldn't believe anything you say even if you swore on your mother's grave."

"My dear Lester. Haven't I always treated you and yours with courtesy and respect? Yet now you treat me as if I'm worse than a red savage. You sadden me. You truly do."

Fargo wondered why none of the farmers had caught on that Gore was stalling. That as Gore talked, Rinson and the other gun sharks were inching their hands toward their pistols and rifles. He went to warn them and once again received a hard jab in the side.

"No talking," Harvey snapped.

Fargo braced for the explosion. The women on the far side of the circle were also prepared for the worst, many with their arms around their frightened children. But not Martha Winston. She looked mad more than anything, and Fargo didn't blame her.

Gore spread his hands. "I'll make one last appeal. Can't we talk this over, Lester? There's enough gold for all of us."

The big farmer took a step nearer. "Enough talk, Victor. Do as I told you."

"What a shame," Gore said sadly, even as his right hand streaked to the revolver tucked under his belt—Fargo's Colt.

"No!" Lester cried, and fired, and bedlam broke out.

The slug caught Gore high in the shoulder. The impact wasn't enough to knock him from the saddle but he left it anyway, diving for the ground. Rinson and Slag and Perkins and the rest stabbed for their weapons. Only a few farmers had the presence of mind to snap off quick shots. The rest were momentarily rooted in shock at the sudden violence. Then guns were booming all over the place, revolvers and rifles and shotguns spewing lead and smoke amid a chaos of curses and screams and shouts.

So much was taking place, so fast, that Fargo couldn't take it all in, and didn't try. He dropped flat as Harvey and the other farmer rushed to the aid of their brethren. Bodies were falling, some motionless, many continuing to squeeze off rounds.

Lester Winston ran up to Gore to finish him off. He never saw Perkins. He probably never heard the shot that blew off the top of his skull in a spectacular shower of gore.

Larson killed one of the women and in turn lost the lower half of his face to a shotgun blast.

Stern raked his spurs and tried to break into the clear,

only to be brought crashing down by several farmers who all fired at the same time.

Screeching horribly, yet another farmer oozed to the earth, his hand clasped to the empty socket where one of his eyeballs had been.

Fargo couldn't just lie there. A stray slug might claim him. Or one of the protectors might spot him and cut loose. He saw Victor Gore scrambling toward the next wagon, and crawled to intercept him. Gore had the Colt in one hand and a spreading stain high on his shirt.

Fargo was almost to him when Gore whipped around and pointed the Colt at his forehead.

"I've got you now, you son of a bitch."

Fargo coiled to spring. He heard the click of the hammer and knew his time had come.

Then suddenly Rachel was there. She jammed the muzzle of her rifle to the back of Gore's head, and fired. Grinning ear to ear, she yelled, "When this is over, you owe me!"

"Look out!" Fargo shouted.

Rachel didn't see Perkins rein his mount up close. His first shot slammed into her side and sent her stumbling against the wagon. His second ripped through her bosom as she tried to turn. Her eyes flicked to Fargo's, mirroring deep sadness, and regret. Then Perkins fired a third time and the heavy lead cored her temple and burst out the other side.

Hot rage exploded in Fargo. He launched himself at her killer. Perkins pointed his revolver but when the hammer fell there was a *click*. The cylinder was empty.

Perkins lunged for a rifle in his saddle scabbard.

By then Fargo reached him. Grabbing a leg, he sent Perkins toppling. But Perkins was up in a crouch in a twinkling, his knife in hand.

That suited Fargo. Drawing the Arkansas toothpick, he sprang. Steel lanced at his neck but he parried and opened Perkins' arm from wrist to elbow. Perkins instantly switched the knife to his other hand and stabbed at Fargo's belly. But Fargo was ready. Shifting, he plunged the toothpick to the hilt in the base of Perkins' throat, then leaped back.

Blood spurted from the wound and gushed from Perkins' mouth. He staggered, tripped, and crashed down. A few convulsions and it was all over.

The thunderous discharge of a shotgun reminded Fargo of the battle being waged all around him. Harvey was dead, drilled through the forehead. A woman had been shot through the heart. One of Rinson's men flopped madly about with part of his face missing.

Fargo scooped up his Colt. As he spun, lead blistered his ear. Rinson was still in the saddle, and took deliberate aim. Fargo was quicker. His hands a blur, he fired from the hip, fanning the hammer. Holes appeared in Rinson's face, in his neck, in his chest.

A blow to the shoulder jarred Fargo to his marrow. He swiveled to find Slag holding a rifle by the barrel, about to swing again. Fargo brought up the Colt, or tried to. His arm wouldn't rise as it should. He was much too slow, and about to have his brains bashed out.

It was then that Martha Winston materialized out of the swirl of gun smoke, a double-barreled shotgun in her hands. She let Slag have both barrels full in the face.

Silence abruptly fell. Fargo's ears rang as he slowly surveyed the slaughter. There was no other word for it.

Blasted, bleeding bodies were everywhere. Victor Gore was dead. All the killers had fallen; Rinson, Perkins, Slag, Larson, Stern, all dead, dead, dead, dead. There wasn't a farmer left standing, either. Lester, Harvey, every last one of them, and the women who had helped them, all blown to hell. Only Martha was left, Martha, and the women and children at the other side of the circle.

"I tried to warn you," Fargo said to the still form of her husband.

A sob escaped Martha. "Dear Lord, no," she said, and shuffled over to Rachel. "Not her, too."

"She saved my life," Fargo said, but he doubted that Martha heard him. Tears trickling down her cheeks, she uttered a loud sob and sank to her knees.

"Not my girl. Please, not my girl."

Fargo's Henry lay partially under Stern, the brass receiver spattered with red drops. Fargo tugged it loose.

Martha stared at him, her eyes pits of horror. "It's not as I thought, is it? All my life, and it's not as I thought."

"It never is," Fargo said.

There wasn't much more.

Fargo offered to take the survivors to Fort Bridger. Martha wanted to bury the dead, but Fargo was anxious to get everyone out of there before the Nez Perce found them. He looked back only once—the sky was thick with buzzards.

Fargo told himself he wasn't going to, but he did. From Fort Bridger he headed straight back to the canyon. He intended to help himself to some of the gold and then treat himself to wild nights of whiskey, women and cards. But the sacks were gone. Every last one. Either the Nez Perce had found them, or Gore and Rinson hid them before heading for the valley and their date with death.

As for the O'Flynns, the family Fargo was searching for when the whole ordeal started, it turned out they had made it to Oregon, after all. The father paid Fargo for finding them, and Fargo promptly sought out the nearest watering hole.

He had a lot of forgetting to do.

LOOKING FORWARD!
The following is the opening
section from the next novel in the exciting
Trailsman series from Signet:

**THE TRAILSMAN #328
TEXAS TRIGGERS**

*The hard land of the Pecos, 1861—
where the Apache reigned, and the
unwary paid for their follies in pain
and blood.*

The sun was killing him.

It hung at its zenith, a blazing yellow furnace. For weeks now, west Texas had been scorched by relentless heat. The land baked, the vegetation withered, the wildlife suffered. It was the worst summer anyone could remember in the desert country west of the Pecos River.

That included Skye Fargo. He had been through Texas before, plenty of times, and he had never experienced heat like this. Heat so hot, his skin felt as if it were on fire. With each breath, he inhaled flame into his lungs. Squinting up at the cause, Fargo summed up his sentiments with a single, bitter "Damn."

His horse was suffering, too. The Ovaro was as good

a mount as a man could ask for. It had stamina to spare, but the merciless heat had boiled its strength away to where the stallion plodded along with its head hung low, so weary and worn that Fargo had commenced to worry. Which was why he was walking and leading the stallion by the reins.

Any man stranded afoot in that country had one foot in the grave. Any man except an Apache.

The Mescaleros had roamed that region since anyone could remember. Tempered by the forge of adversity, they prowled in search of prey. The heat didn't affect their iron constitutions. And, too, they knew all the secret water holes and tanks. They thrived where most whites would perish.

Most, but not all. The harsh land of cactus, mesquite and limestone rock was home to scattered settlers. Isolated valleys amid the maze of canyons and plateaus where pockets of green against the backdrop of brown. But not this summer. Now most of those green valleys were as brown as everything else.

It was just Fargo's luck to be passing through after delivering a dispatch to Fort Davis. He was on his own, and headed for cooler climes. The sun, though, was doing its best to roast him and the Ovaro alive, and it was close to succeeding.

Fargo stopped and gazed out over the bleak, blistered landscape. He licked his cracked lips. Or tried to. His mouth was as dry as the rest of him, and he had no spit to spare. He glanced back at the Ovaro. "Hold on, boy. I'll find us water if it's the last thing I do."

It might well be.

Broad of shoulder and narrow of waist, Skye Fargo was all muscle and whipcord. He wore buckskins and boots and a white hat made brown by dust. Around his neck was a splash of color: a red bandanna. At his hip hung a Colt. In an ankle sheath inside his boot was an

Arkansas toothpick. From the saddle jutted the stock of a Henry rifle.

At first glance, Fargo looked no different from most frontiersmen. But he had more experience in the wild than any ten of them put together. In his travels he had been most everywhere, seen most everything. He'd lived with Indians and knew their ways. In short, if any white could make it through that country, Fargo could.

Or so he thought when he started out. Now he wasn't so sure.

Fargo tried to swallow, and couldn't. He ran a hand across his hot brow and was surprised at how little sweat there was. He had little moisture left in him. His body was a cloth wrung dry, and unless he found water, and found it soon, his bleached bones would join the many skeletons that already littered the desert.

Fargo had to force his legs to move. A bad sign, that. His body was giving out. The steely sinews that had served him in such good stead had turned traitor and would not do as he wanted unless he lashed them with the whip of his will.

The Ovaro went a short way and abruptly stopped.

Fargo tugged on the reins to keep the pinto moving but it didn't respond. He turned, and saw that it had its head up and its ears pricked, and it was staring fixedly to one side. He looked and saw nothing but boulders and dirt and a few brown bushes and tufts of brown grass.

"There's nothing there. Come on." Fargo gave another tug and the Ovaro plodded after him, but it kept staring and its nostrils flared.

Belatedly, Fargo's heat-dulled mind realized that something was out there. Or, more likely, *someone*. No animal would be abroad in that heat. And since there wasn't another white within miles, so far as Fargo knew, that left the last ones Fargo wanted to meet up with.

That left the Mescalero Apaches.

Fargo was in no shape for a fight. Alert now, he watched from under his hat brim but saw nothing to account for the Ovaro's interest. He was about convinced the stallion was mistaken when a hint of movement sent a tingle of alarm down his spine.

He was being stalked.

Outwardly, Fargo stayed calm. He mustn't let on that he knew. He kept on walking, his right arm at his side, his hand brushing his Colt. It would help if he had some idea how many were shadowing him but that was like counting ghosts. Fargo wondered why they hadn't attacked yet. It could be they were waiting for the heat to weaken him even more. Or maybe there was a spot up ahead better fitted for an ambush.

Ordinarily, Fargo would have swung onto the Ovaro and used his spurs. But the stallion was in no shape for a hard ride. He doubted it would last half a mile without collapsing. And then the Apaches would have him.

Fargo racked his brain. His best bet was to lure them in close where he could drop them with his Colt. But Apaches weren't stupid. They wouldn't fall for whatever trick he tried unless it was convincing.

Then it hit him. The answer was in the sky above. He squinted up at the sun again, and made a show of running his sleeve across his face. He wanted the Apaches to think he was about done in. True, he was, but he still had a spark of vitality left, and that spark might save his hide.

Before him the country flattened. In the distance were some hills.

Fargo stopped and gazed idly about, then moved toward a large cactus. It offered hardly any shade but he plopped down in what shade there was and sat with his head hung and his shoulders slumped to the give the impression he just couldn't go on.

Other than cactus, the spot Fargo had chosen was

open. No one, not even a wily Apache, could get at him without him seeing. They might come in a rush but only after he collapsed. And that's exactly what he did. He put his left hand under him as if he were so weak he could barely sit up. He stayed like that a while, then let his elbow bend and slowly sank onto his side. From where he lay he could see his back trail but not much to either side. He could see the Ovaro, though, and that was what counted.

For the longest while nothing happened.

The heat seeped into Fargo's bones, into his very marrow. He began to feel sleepy and almost gave a toss of his head to shake the lethargy off. But that would give him away. Struggling to keep his senses sharp, he saw the Ovaro lift its head and stare to the north. Fargo shifted his gaze in that direction but his hat brim hid whatever was out there.

Fargo seldom felt so vulnerable, so exposed. He slowly shifted his cheek so he could see past the brim. All he saw were cactus. Yet the Ovaro was still staring.

Where were they? Fargo wondered. Apaches were masters at blending in. They could literally hide in plain sight. Once, years ago, he met an Apache scout who showed him how. They had been standing in open country, and the Apache had him turn his back and count to ten. When he turned around, the man was gone. Fargo had been stumped and called out to him, and the Apache, grinning, rose from behind a bush no bigger than a breadbasket where he had dug a shallow hole and covered himself, all in the blink of an eye.

Damned impressive, that little demonstration.

Fargo searched the vicinity but saw nothing. He looked so long and so hard that his eyes started to smart. He decided to watch the Ovaro instead, thinking the stallion would react once the warriors were close enough. It wasn't staring to the north anymore. It was staring at something *behind* him.

Fargo's skin crawled. At any moment he might get an arrow or a knife in the back. He was sorely tempted to roll over but if he did the warrior would melt away.

It was a nightmare, lying there waiting for something to happen. Fargo's nerves jangled like a shriek of fire in a theater. The taut seconds stretched into a minute and the minute into two, and it was a wonder he didn't snap and leap to his feet.

Then the Ovaro nickered and stamped a heavy hoof.

Fargo rolled over, drawing the Colt as he moved. It was safe to say the Apache a few feet away with a knife in hand was considerably surprised but he recovered quickly. The bronzed warrior sprang, the steel of his blade glinting in the sunlight.

Flat on his back, Fargo fanned the Colt twice. At that range he could hardly miss. Both slugs caught the Apache high in the chest and twisted him half around. Baring his teeth, he got a hand under him and levered forward, seeking to bury his knife with his dying breath. The tip was inches from Fargo when the warrior collapsed, sprawling forward on his belly so that his forearm ended up across Fargo. Pushing it off, Fargo heaved erect and spun, braced for an onslaught of war whoops and weapons.

There were no outcries. No other warriors appeared.

Fargo kept turning from side to side. Finally he admitted the obvious. The one he had shot was the only one. With the toe of his boot he rolled the dead warrior over. The dark eyes were open; they betrayed no shock or fear.

Fargo had no strength to bury him, and no desire to do it even if he had the strength. The man had tried to kill him. Let the buzzards and coyotes gorge. He replaced the spent cartridges, slid the Colt into his holster, and patted the Ovaro. "You saved my skin again. Now let's see if I can save us from dying of thirst."

The distant brown hills held little promise. The drought

had dried up all the streams and it was doubtful he would find one flowing.

Fargo's boots were so hot, it felt as if his feet were being cooked. But he refused to give up. It wasn't in him. So long as he had breath he would resist oblivion with all that he was. He liked living too much. He liked to roam the wild places. He liked whiskey. He liked cards and women. He liked women a lot. An hour or two of passion reminded a man why it was good to be alive.

Fargo chuckled, but the sound that came from his parched throat was more like the rattle of seeds in a dry gourd. "God, I need water," he rasped, and it hurt to speak.

The hills grew near. By late afternoon Fargo was among them. And as he had feared, it was more of the same. More endless dry. In all that vast inferno, the only living creatures were the Ovaro and him. Not a single bird was in the air. He had not seen a lizard or snake all day. The scrape of his boots and the thud of the Ovaro's hooves were the only sounds.

Fargo's chin drooped. His blood felt as if it were boiling in his veins. He would gladly find a patch of shade and rest, but he honestly didn't know if he could get back up again.

The sun dipped toward the horizon. Once it set, the night would bring welcome relief. But without water it would be fleeting, at best.

His legs leaden, Fargo shuffled grimly on. He nearly lost his hold on the reins when the Ovaro unexpectedly stopped.

"What the hell?"

Turning, Fargo pulled but the Ovaro refused to move. Its head was up and it was staring straight ahead.

Thinking it was another Apache, Fargo spun, his hand dropping to his Colt. But it wasn't a warrior out to do him in.

It was a cow.

Not a longhorn or a steer or a bull but an honest-to-God milk cow, calmly regarding him from fifty feet away while chewing its cud.

Fargo blinked, certain he must be seeing things. "You would think it would be a naked woman."

The cow flicked its ears.

That was when Fargo noticed the tiny bell that dangled from a rawhide cord around its neck. Unless he missed his guess, the cow was a Jersey. He seemed to recollect that the breed got its start on an island of that name somewhere, long ago, but where he picked up that tidbit he had no idea. The kind of cow didn't really matter. It shouldn't be there. And yet it was.

"Pleased to meet you, madam."

The cow went on chewing.

Fargo moved toward it, talking quietly. "Do you live around here? I'd like to meet whoever milks you and ask for some of your milk or some water." Anything to slake his thrist.

Slowly turning, the cow lumbered off along the bottom of a hill. She was thick with flies, and a swish of her tail sent them buzzing.

Fargo followed. He couldn't believe his luck. To have stumbled on a ranch in the middle of nowhere! Although now that he thought about it, he recollected there were a few hardy souls in those parts. Fools, a lot of folks called them, for daring to put down roots in the heart of Apache territory. No one in their right mind would do such a thing.

The cow was out of sight around the hill.

Anxious to catch up, Fargo stepped into the stirrups. "Sorry," he said to the Ovaro. The stallion apparently smelled or sensed their salvation and needed no urging. It moved before he could tap his spurs. He half feared he would get to the other side of the hill and the cow wouldn't be there, that it really was his overheated mind playing tricks on him.

Excerpt from TEXAS TRIGGERS

Then a valley spread before him, a brown valley, a valley as dry as the hills and the desert. And there was the Jersey cow, moving out across a well-worn trail that led to the far end.

Fargo was so intent on the cow that he didn't pay much attention to the hill they had just come around. He realized his mistake when he heard a metallic click. Instinctively, he threw himself from the saddle just as a rifle thundered. He landed on his shoulder and rolled onto his belly. Thinking he had several seconds to locate the shooter, he raised his head. But he was wrong. The rifle boomed again, and yet a third time, and miniature dirt geysers came straight toward his face.

No other series packs this much heat!

THE TRAILSMAN

**Follow the trail of the gun-slinging heroes of
Penguin's Action Westerns at
penguin.com/actionwesterns**